Jimi & Isaac 2a:
Keystone Species

Phil Rink

Summary:

Jimi and Isaac are rock stars, epic heroes, intellectuals, and loving sons. They are wise and foolish, sublime and earthy. They are middle-school boys.

Jimi and Isaac think they're going on a boat ride. A simple vacation with Jimi's uncle Tim. But hanging around with Uncle Tim is rarely simple.

Soon it's up to Jimi and Isaac to get things fixed.

ISBN-10: 1499137710
ISBN-13: 978-1499137712

Look for us on the web.
Look for us at Amazon.com.
Get a copy for your Kindle or Kindle App.
Ask for us at your favorite bookstore.
Beg your librarian to buy lots of our books.
Look for us on facebook.
We're not that hard to find.
Secrets are old-fashioned.
You only need secrets if you're buying a birthday
present for your mom, and you want her to have a nice
surprise because she's put up with you for your whole
life and that's not very easy to do.

For Teachers and Helicopter Parents:
28,000 words.
Flesch Reading Ease: 90.6%.
Flesch-Kincaid Grade Level: 2.8.

Lots of ideas to discuss.

*Dedicated to those who wander
above the sea of fog.*

Chapter 1:
At the Airport.

Mom was crying. Blubbering, almost. Like we were babies.

"You boys be safe," she said, wiping her nose with a tissue. "Stay together all the time. Watch out for each other." She wiped her eyes with the backs of her hands. Then she hugged me really tight and then she hugged Isaac, which freaked him out. Isaac isn't really that interested in getting hugs. He certainly isn't interested in hugging back.

She finally let go of Isaac, stepped back, and wiped her eyes with the palms of her hands. Then she blew her nose into her tissue. Snot-o-Rama. She was going to need more tissue.

"We're just flying to Seattle," I said. "People fly on airplanes all the time, and nobody is afraid of Seattle. It's safer than our living room." Our living room is pretty safe. There have been no deaths there that I know of. I guess Seattle might be a little more dangerous than our living room.

"And a boat trip," Isaac added. "Fishing and killer whales and seagulls. Hardly anybody dies on boats. The ocean is a really safe place."

Mom looked at Isaac and smiled a little, crinkling the corners of her bright red eyes. She knew he was trying to help. "Isaac, I'm sorry your parents couldn't come to the airport with us," she said, "but I know you'll be fine, and I know my brother will take good care of you."

Then she blew her nose again. There was a complete tissue failure. Mom's hands were totally full of snot. She had to go to the bathroom to wash.

Dad looked at his feet for a while, then finally he looked up at us.

"Look, boys," Dad said. "Timonius is a good guy. You're going to have a great time with him."

Then Dad opened and closed his mouth a few times, like a fish. Finally he started again.

"But he isn't used to boys, and he's not used to strangers. Just do what you're told for the first few days, get off to a good start, and everything will go great. It's only a two-week trip."

Dad gave me a real serious look.

"Who's Timonius?" I asked.

"Just a nickname," Dad said. "Forget I brought it up. His name is Tim. Uncle Tim."

"You"—he grabbed Isaac by the shoulder—"can call him Uncle Tim, too."

"That's good you told me that," Isaac said, "because I was going to call him Uncle Tim One."

Dad let go of Isaac's shoulder.

"Don't worry, Dad," I said, with my best "don't worry" smile. "Uncle Tim and I get along great. It doesn't bother me at all when he yells."

Dad smiled. Then he looked at Isaac.

Isaac was looking past my dad at a little airport store. Dad just waited.

Finally Isaac leaned back a little and looked at Dad. You could see his eyes work back in time until he snapped back into reality.

"No big deal," he said. "I get along with everybody."

Dad and I tried not to laugh. Dad didn't try very hard.

Mom came back from the bathroom as they announced early boarding. She just smiled her best fake smile and hugged us again and told me she loved me and told me to be safe and watch out for Isaac and told Isaac she loved him and to watch out for me and told us to stay together and to watch out for each other and then she hugged us again.

Then the airplane people walked us down the hallway thing to the airplane.

"Tell Janis to stay out of my room!" I yelled, but I wasn't sure if Mom and Dad heard me. Janis is my big sister. She has a problem with boundaries.

Chapter 2:
On the Road.

The yellow zone was for loading and unloading only, which was what we were doing. There was some yelling also.

"What's this?" Uncle Tim yelled.

He probably didn't think he was yelling, but he was yelling.

"Where are we going to put this?" he yelled again.

He was holding Isaac's great big green suitcase, and he had a point. When he talked to Isaac and me about sailing on his boat, he was real clear that we needed to pack our stuff into duffel bags or sacks or something small that packs small. No huge suitcases. He was really clear about that.

"I told you guys no suitcases," he yelled.

"It's not a big deal," Isaac said. "I'll just hold it in my lap."

Uncle Tim stared at Isaac for two seconds, then turned and opened the back passenger door of his car. Both doors on the passenger side were brown with gray around the edges. They didn't look very good on the yellow car. Uncle Tim probably should have painted both doors completely gray instead of just the edges. Anyway, the backseat was completely full of food and paper towels and stuff. There was one of those enormous packs of toilet paper, too.

"You two are going to have to share the front seat," Tim said. "I spent all morning filling the car with provisions and gear for the trip."

"Then we'll just put it in the trunk," Isaac said, like he knew what he was talking about.

Uncle Tim walked to the back of his car and opened the trunk lid. The trunk was completely full of rope and plastic bags and what looked like greasy car parts. Uncle Tim reached underneath a pile of green string, which was actually a net, I think, and pulled out a loop of rope. Then he grabbed my duffel bag and jammed it into the back corner over the taillight. He had to punch it a few times so it didn't stick up.

He untangled the rope and laid it across the back of his car, then shut the trunk lid over the rope. Then he grabbed Isaac's suitcase and tied it over the trunk lid. It didn't really look like it was going to stay there very long.

"Get in the front," he said, "both of you."

Isaac opened the passenger door. "There's only one seat belt," he whined.

"You can share it," Uncle Tim said. "Or you can let Jimi wear it alone, if you want."

Isaac and I tried to sit side by side on the front seat but the seat was too narrow. By the time we were out of the airport, I was sitting on his lap, with the seat belt across both of us. It was completely weird.

"This is weird," I told Uncle Tim.

"It's probably illegal, too," Isaac said. "We'll go to jail. We'll be convicts."

"Yeah," Uncle Tim said, "that's the way it is now. Just about everything a man does is illegal. But it can't be helped. I got a call late last night that changes our plans, so I spent all morning rounding up what we need. I know we talked about an easy two weeks lying at anchor, but we're going to sea, instead. You boys will be real sailors by the time we get back."

That didn't sound very good actually.

"Ummm..." I said.

"Don't worry," Uncle Tim said, smiling. "A sound ship is safer at sea than at anchor. No rocks to crash into. No idiots to ram you. No ferries to avoid."

Jimi & Isaac 2a:

"We should call Mom," I said, "since the plan changed."

Uncle Tim glanced at me, then looked back at the road. Traffic was pretty bad. "Yeah," he said, "we should. We'll call her when we get to the boat."

"How long will that be?" Isaac asked, pushing me over so I was sitting on his other leg. "Soon, I hope."

Uncle Tim checked his watch. "Four hours."

Isaac groaned. "You're kidding, right? We can't do this for four hours!"

He was right, but he was pretty whiny. I don't think Uncle Tim wanted to be in the car with us for that long either.

"We'll be at the boat in four hours," Uncle Tim said, "but before that we'll be at the ferry landing in just over an hour. Then we can get out of the car. We'll get the car in line and wait for the ferry for almost an hour, then ride the ferry for just over two hours, then we'll be at the boat. We'll head to sea at first light tomorrow."

Isaac inhaled real loud, like he was winding up for a tantrum, so I tried to change it up.

"Where are we headed?" I asked. "When we go to sea, I mean." It seemed like a pretty good question too, once I said it out loud. Serious and interested.

Uncle Tim thought for a little bit.

"That," he said, "is a good question. You'll have to wait and see."

Isaac and I found a couple of bench seats on the ferry and slept for the whole ride, then Uncle Tim woke us up so we could get back in the car.

"When we get to the boat," Uncle Tim said, "we'll just unload the car right next to the gate and you guys can pack everything down. I need to get one more load of groceries. You two look like you might eat more than I planned for."

"Count on it," Isaac said. "Eat and grow, grow and eat. Jimi the stick needs it more than me."

Since I was sitting on Isaac's lap, there wasn't much I could say, really. I just tried to sit heavier.

"We don't know where anything goes," I said. "On your boat. We don't know where to put—"

"No big deal," Uncle Tim answered.

He started the motor and drove off the ferry. There was a guy in an orange vest directing traffic, waving us ahead. He looked at Isaac and me in the front seat, but didn't arrest us or anything.

"I'll help you with the first load," Uncle Tim said. "Show you the boat and open it up. Then you two can just load everything into the saloon. We'll put it away later."

"I was reading about boats," Isaac said.

This should be good. Uncle Tim just waited. He was starting to get used to Isaac, I think.

"The main room in a boat is a salon," Isaac finished.

"My boat's main cabin is a saloon," Uncle Tim answered.

I think he had been through this word choice issue before. Maybe he started it on purpose.

"A salon is where women get their hair styled."

Yep. He started it on purpose.

It was a really short drive to the parking lot at the marina where all the boats were. Isaac and I should have walked. Uncle Tim was probably worried we'd get lost, though, since we didn't know anything about anything. I just knew I didn't want to sit on Isaac's lap anymore. The entire drive from getting off the ferry to parking at the boat place was surrounded by tall, tall evergreen trees that blocked out the sky everywhere but straight overhead. It was like we were in a tiny green room with a tall blue ceiling.

We unloaded the backseat and the car's trunk onto the sidewalk.

Thousands or millions of boats were tied to walkways that floated in the water. The boats were like houses and the sidewalks were like streets, but the boats were real close to each other. Like a parking lot, I guess. It looked crowded to me. The boat parking lot is called a marina. I don't know why they use Spanish. They should call it a boatery. Shipiteria. Waterlot, maybe.

"Load up," Uncle Tim said. "Let's get this done."

Isaac grabbed his great big green suitcase.

"Not that!"

Isaac looked up.

"Bad enough we brought it this far. No way it goes on the boat."

Isaac scrunched his forehead so hard it made his eyebrows touch.

Uncle Tim reached into a pile of rags and pulled out a big orange bed sheet. He wadded it up and tossed it to Isaac. "Use this. You can put it on your bunk after you get your clothes stowed."

Isaac dumped the clothes from his suitcase into the sheet and twisted the corners together into a sack, like those old-time movie hobos. The suitcase was almost empty, too. That made Uncle Tim mad again. Isaac had only packed one extra pair of pants, two shirts, and ten pairs of underwear. "Personal hygiene matters," Isaac said. He had a bunch of socks, too.

The great big green suitcase went into Uncle Tim's backseat.

Chapter 3:
Reality Checkout.

Uncle Tim's boat was named *DUCK*. We could tell because the word *DUCK* was painted in red letters with blue outlining on the back end. Painted like by a five-year-old painted. The blue paint even had drips.

"Who painted your boat name?" Isaac asked.

"Shut up," Uncle Tim said. "Get your gear on the boat."

I climbed up on the *DUCK* and over the metal railing, and then Isaac handed me our clothes and Uncle Tim's gear. Then I carried it all to the bench seats in the middle of the boat.

"Just put it there in the cockpit," Uncle Tim said. "I'll open the companionway in a second."

So I guess the seats were the cockpit, and the companionway was probably where the wood doors were at the front of the cockpit.

"Where are the sails?" Isaac asked.

I looked up. Yup, there was a big metal sailboat mast but no sails. The other sailboats in the marina had sails and ropes and more ropes. I don't know the right names for the parts.

"No sails," Uncle Tim said, sliding back a cover and pulling out some wood boards that blocked the way into the boat. "This used to be a sailboat. Now it's a powerboat with a vestigial mast. New sails are really expensive, the wind never blows the right way when you need it, and sailboats make really good powerboats, because they have efficient hulls. Now get the rest of the gear down below. I've got one more stop at one more store, then I'll pick up some dinner and I'll be back in just a few."

And he disappeared.

Uncle Tim got back quicker than we thought. Just in time, too.

"I have to pee," Isaac said. "Where's the bathroom?"

"Sure," Uncle Tim said. "Follow me."

"You can just point," Isaac said. "I don't need help."

Uncle Tim kept going. "You, too, Jimi," he yelled over his shoulder. "You both need to know about this."

Jimi & Isaac 2a:

I didn't think I needed to know about Isaac going pee, but I followed Isaac anyway. Two steps down from the saloon, under the windows, was a skinny door off to the right. Uncle Tim opened the door and stepped into the tiny little bathroom. Isaac jammed into the doorway, and I stayed upstairs and looked over Isaac's shoulder.

"Jimi, can you see?" Uncle Tim said, looking up at me past Isaac's ear.

"I really have to go," Isaac said. He was starting to dance a little.

"Let me show you how to work the head, then you'll be fine," Uncle Tim said. He was standing next to a tiny little toilet. Right next to him was an even smaller sink. It was like a toy bathroom. "Boats don't have bathrooms; they have heads. That's because the old-time sailing ships always sailed downwind, and they would do their business—"

"I really have to go," Isaac said, still dancing.

"Fine. OK. First you set this lever here to the left, pump the handle a few times to put some water into the bowl, and then pee or poop or whatever. When you're done, pump the handle, bringing more water in and pumping the waste overboard, until the water in the bowl is clear. Then move the lever to the right..."

There was a click, but I couldn't see the lever. I figured now was not the time to ask questions. Isaac was really hopping around.

"...and pump the bowl dry."

"Can you move, please?" Isaac was really in trouble.

"For now, use the toilets on the shore if you need to poop. Don't make a mess in the water at the dock. At sea it's fine."

"Please move," Isaac said.

"It's actually illegal for us to pump sewage overboard and we can be fined if we're caught, so use the toilets on shore if you need to poop, except at night. Don't stink up the dock while people are around. Got it?"

Isaac actually pulled Uncle Tim out of the room and slammed the door. Uncle Tim looked surprised.

"I think he got it," I said.

Chapter 4:
Say What?

We had pizza for dinner. Good pizza, too.

"Why does that surprise you?" Uncle Tim asked. "Did you think we'd be eating beans out of the can?"

"I thought we'd eat fish," Isaac said. "Like the Pacific Coast Indians. Smoked salmon, salted cod. Fish for breakfast, fish for lunch, fish for dinner."

Uncle Tim just looked at him. He didn't answer. Sometimes that's the best way to deal with Isaac.

Sometimes it doesn't work, though.

"Where are all the Indians?" Isaac asked. "Where are the totem poles and the longhouses and war canoes and —"

"The Indians," Uncle Tim said, standing up from the table and collecting the paper plates and the empty pizza box into a big green trash bag, "are probably at home eating pizza."

He twisted the top of the bag shut and tied it into a knot, then held it out to Isaac.

"Take this up to the trash can at the top of the dock," he said, "and make sure you get the lid shut when you're done. We have way too many raccoons hanging around. People need to stop feeding them."

Isaac slid out from behind the table, grabbed the bag, and turned for the companionway. Then he stopped. More like he turned into a statue. A statue with its mouth open.

There was a lady in the companionway. Her round face and dark skin made her eyes look huge and shiny. Her black hair was braided into one long braid that hung over her shoulder, almost to her waist. She was really, really pretty. Really pretty. No wonder Isaac was stuck.

He got over it, though.

"Are you an Indian?" he asked.

What an idiot.

Her eyes got really narrow, and she stared at Isaac as she stepped down the stairs into the saloon. I mean really stared. Her eyes never moved.

She stopped on the last step so her eyes were even with Isaac's and leaned into his face, nose-to-nose. Isaac tried to back up, but there wasn't room.

"Why do you want to know?" she asked quietly. "Are you a cowboy?"

Uncle Tim exploded. I've never heard anyone laugh so hard in one shot.

The lady smiled and slid past Isaac. She got herself a glass of water and leaned against the counter. Isaac still hadn't moved.

"Boys," Uncle Tim said finally, when he stopped giggling, "this is Mary. She'll be with us for the first part of our trip."

"Mary," he continued, pointing with his open hand, palm up, "this is my nephew Jimi"—she nodded at me—"and his friend Isaac."

Isaac turned a little and waved in the most stupid possible way. He was only a few feet from her.

"Not a cowboy?" she said, glancing at Uncle Tim.

Isaac didn't answer.

"Not a cowboy," Uncle Tim said.

"Well, Isaac," Mary said, "the first thing you need to know is we don't really use the word 'Indian' very often. We say 'Native American' or 'indigenous population' or 'tribal group' or 'band,' all of which"—she paused with her hand in the air—"are awkward. In Canada, they say 'First Nation.' 'Indian' came from Columbus. He's not too relevant up here. Usually, though, when you meet an actual"—she said "actual" like it had twenty-seven letters that were all capitals—"Indian, they would probably prefer that you use their name, not their category."

"The second thing you need to know," she said, taking a sip of her water, "is that I was born on Hawaii —the big island. Ethnically, I am a Pacific Islander. So, following the pattern we've discussed, you would refer to me as 'Mary.'"

Uncle Tim was still smiling.

"Go, Isaac. Escape while you can," he said.

Isaac was off the boat in a second. He dawdled at the trash can, too. Probably a good idea.

Isaac and I slept on shelves way in the front end of the boat.

"Bunks," Uncle Tim said. "Like bunk beds. Or you can call them berths."

Whatever.

"It's like a secret language," Isaac said. "Beds are berths, rooms are cabins, doors are companionways, windows are portlights, floors are decks, stairs are ladders."

"Yeah, secret," I said. I was getting kind of tired. "No point in using the perfectly good words we already have."

Isaac took the top shelf. I didn't mind. I could sit on my bed to get dressed or put my shoes on. Isaac had to stand in the only little tiny clear space. He stepped on me climbing into his bunk, though. Jerk.

Chapter 5:
The Safety Tour.

When I woke up the next morning, I could hear running water. A lot of running water. I had been dreaming of camping next to a river with my dad, so I was confused for a while. But then I figured it out.

The boat was sinking!

"Isaac! Get up!" I yelled. "We're sinking!"

He leaned over the side of his berth. His huge head looked like the moon rising over a mountain range.

"Not likely," he mumbled. "The engine is running. It's been running for a while. How do you sleep through noise like that?"

I lay back down and was quiet for a while. Isaac was right; the engine was running. It was actually pretty loud, but it was such an even noise it was easy to ignore. Like when it's windy in the woods, eventually you don't hear the wind. The water noise still freaked me out, though. It was coming from right next to my head.

"There must be some sort of pipe in this wall," I told Isaac. "I can hear water running."

Isaac leaned over the edge of his bunk again. The man in the moon had a great big toothy smile.

"Yeah," he said, "a pipe. Wake up, Jimi. The water's not moving; *we're* moving."

Then I did freak out a little. My head was only six inches or so from the ocean. The side of the boat was so thin that it sounded like it wasn't even there.

Mary was sitting at the table, sipping a cup of coffee and sewing on a little piece of fabric she had in a wooden hoop. I looked up the companionway into the cockpit, but I didn't see Uncle Tim. I could see the trees on the shore way over to our left but only water in the other directions. The sun was coming up, sparkling in the foamy water behind us. The wheel was turning back and forth, just a little bit, but nobody was there to turn it.

"Who's driving?" I asked Mary.

"The autopilot," she said, looking over the top of her stitching and showing me a little gray box by her left hand. "We just set a compass course, and the autopilot steers the boat in a straight line."

Oh. Wow.

"Where's Uncle Tim?"

Mary opened her mouth to answer, but then the floor tipped and the engine noise got a lot louder. I stepped back to a part of the floor that wasn't moving.

The piece of floor flipped up, and there was Uncle Tim.

I started to tell him "good morning," but it was too loud. I didn't want to yell.

He put his hands on the floor, scooted up onto his butt, and then swung his legs out of the hole.

When he shut the trapdoor, the engine noise almost went away.

"Good morning, nephew Jimi with an 'i'!" Uncle Tim said. He was maybe happier than I've ever seen him.

"That's the engine room," he said, pointing at his feet. "I'll take you and Isaac down later and show you around."

"Right after breakfast," Isaac yelled, right behind my ear. "I'll cook the oatmeal!"

Isaac was all happy, too. I didn't get it. I just wanted to sleep a little more.

Isaac's oatmeal was actually not terrible. I had raisins and milk in mine; he had brown sugar and raisins and milk. Uncle Tim and Mary just had more coffee. Maybe

they ate before they cast off or launched or left the dock
or whatever you call it when you leave in a boat.

"OK, Jimi," Uncle Tim said. "Isaac cooked, so you
get the dishes done, then we'll do our safety tour."

Isaac's cooking was just tearing the instant oatmeal
bags open and pouring boiling water, but fine. I did the
dishes.

Uncle Tim took us forward and showed us the fire
extinguisher in our cabin, and then we moved
backwards, which is called aft, and saw the fire
extinguisher in the saloon, which was also the fire
extinguisher for the galley, then we moved farther aft
and saw the fire extinguisher for the Uncle Tim's cabin.

"Now, put these on," Uncle Tim said. He handed us
each a pair of earmuffs made of hard plastic. "They're
hearing protectors, for the engine room."

"You weren't wearing these," I said, "when you were
in the engine room." They looked pretty horrible. I
figured they'd probably squeeze my head like a melon
and squish my brains.

"Your mother doesn't care if I go deaf," he said. "I
promised her you'd wear these."

Isaac had his hearing protectors on already. "Wow,"
he shouted, "these are great!" He had a big grin on his
face.

"You don't need to shout," Uncle Tim said. "The
muffs don't block voices as much as they block engine
noises. We can talk in our normal voices."

Jimi & Isaac 2a:

I put mine on, and we dropped through the trapdoor in the floor. Uncle Tim went in first, then Isaac pushed past me and dropped in, then I got in. I left the trapdoor open so I could get out again if I needed to.

The engine room was actually much bigger than I thought it would be. Everything, including the engine, was painted white. The engine was right in the middle of the room. There was a belt and pulleys on the front, just like on a car motor, and a big steel tube came out the back end. The tube was spinning like crazy.

"Don't touch that," Uncle Tim said. He was talking a little louder than normal but not shouting. I could hear him just fine. "That's the prop shaft. It's turning the propeller."

"Port and starboard fuel tanks," he didn't yell, pointing to the left and right edges of the engine room. "Fifty-five gallons each. You check the levels here"— and he pointed at some clear pipes running vertically at the front of each tank—"in these sight glasses."

The left tank, which was the port tank, I guess, must have been completely full because the tube was completely red. The starboard tank was almost full. The red liquid almost filled the tube.

"Is that gas?" Isaac asked. He had to ask a few times until he talked loud enough for Uncle Tim to hear him. The ear protectors were tricky.

"Diesel fuel," Uncle Tim said. "Like gasoline but more oily. Here are the fuel filters, always check them for clean fuel and no water."

The fuel filters were clear bowls filled with the same red liquid as the sight glasses on the tanks. Which made sense, I suppose. Valves next to the filters let you choose which tank of fuel to use.

"These are the drinking water tanks," Uncle Tim said, pointing. "Seventy-five gallons per side."

The water tanks looked just like the fuel tanks, except they covered the back wall of the engine room and the liquid in the sight glasses was clear. There were valves at the bottom of each tank, with hoses running to a black box on the wall.

"Potable water pump," Uncle Tim said when I pointed at the black box and made a question with my eyebrows.

Then Uncle Tim showed us how to check the engine oil, which was a dipstick just like in a car except I've never checked the oil in a car with the engine running. Then he showed us where the extra engine coolant and motor oil were stored.

"So that was the engine room," Uncle Tim said, closing the trapdoor after we'd all climbed out. "Nothing magic. If we keep the motor full of oil and give it plenty of clean fuel, it will run forever."

That seemed unlikely. Nothing runs forever.

"Any questions?" Uncle Tim asked.

Jimi & Isaac 2a:

Isaac took his ear protectors off. "I don't learn too well by listening," he said.

That made me laugh. "Duh," I said.

Isaac gave me a look.

"I'd rather learn by reading."

"No worries," Uncle Tim said. He reached past Mary, who didn't even look up from her sewing, and grabbed a big red-and-orange book off the shelf behind her. He handed it to Isaac.

"Chapter eight is about engines," Uncle Tim said, "but this book covers everything on the boat."

"Cool," said Isaac. He opened the book and started forward, to our cabin.

"Wait," Uncle Tim said, "there's one more thing I promised Jimi's mom." He reached into a cabinet under the dinette seats and pulled out two life jackets. They were the cool spongy foam kind and they looked brand-new. "You guys wear these whenever you're on deck," he said. "No exceptions, ever."

"We didn't wear them last night," Isaac said.

"Whenever you're on deck, and we're not tied to a dock."

Isaac shrugged his shoulders and took his book forward.

Uncle Tim looked at me and plopped the life jackets on the dinette seat. I handed him my ear protectors.

"Sure," I said.

Then I thought of something.

"Did you call my mom to tell her our plans changed?" I asked.

Mary stopped sewing and looked at Uncle Tim. Her eyes were big and round again.

"Oops," Uncle Tim said. "I'll take care of that later."

Mary looked at him some more.

"Later today."

She went back to her sewing.

Chapter 6:
Fishing.

Uncle Tim took a quick look around the boat, peeked into the engine room, stuck his head outside, and looked around, then ducked back into the saloon.

"Right!" he said, clapping his hands together. "Jimi, you have the con!" Then he ducked into his cabin and shut the door.

I had the con. I looked at Mary. She was still sewing. "What's a con?" I said.

"He means," she said, handing me the gray box for the autopilot, "it's your fault."

"What's my fault?" I didn't like the sound of this.

"Everything. Anything. You are in control of this vessel. It's your responsibility. Until you give control to someone else and they take it, you're in charge."

I took the autopilot control from Mary. It had a big round knob in the center, and a little electronic display above the big round knob, and several little switches underneath the big round knob. I didn't recognize any of the words on the switches.

I took the controller and sat next to Mary. That didn't really seem to help much, except I could see out the front windows. That was probably good, I thought, to be able to see where I was going. I didn't know where we were going, though. Uncle Tim didn't say to turn or anything. I got up and stuck my head out of the companionway so I could see behind us. Our wake, the foam and waves the boat makes, was spread out behind us. We hadn't turned in a long time. So we probably wouldn't turn again for a while, I figured.

I sat down next to Mary again.

"Do you know what you're doing?" she asked, still sewing.

"I think so," I said, "I'll just keep the boat going straight and look…"

She had stopped sewing and was looking at me. "No?"

"So," she said, holding her needle ready to make the next stitch but not moving, "if you're in charge but you don't know what to do, what's the first thing you need to do?"

That was a pretty good question. "I don't know," I said.

"It seems to me," she said, putting the needle into the fabric then putting the fabric and hoop onto the table, "that if you don't know what you need to do, the first thing you need to do is find out what you need to do."

That was a pretty complicated sentence, but I agreed with her. I didn't know what to do.

"I should talk to Uncle Tim?" I said.

"Your uncle Tim shut the door to his cabin. That was probably a hint."

"I wonder if that book that Isaac is reading has stuff on being the con," I said.

"Having the con," she said. "Having the controls. Being a con is something else entirely."

I just shrugged.

"Do you have time to read a book?" Mary asked. Then she smiled a little.

Got it. "Mary," I said, "would you please show me what I'm supposed to be doing?"

"Jimi," she said, smiling big-time, "I'd be happy to."

It wasn't complicated to be in control. I just needed to know the plan. Mary showed me the chart plotter, an electronic map that had our course, or plan, drawn in green and our path in red.

Mary said the red line was our "bread crumbs" line, like if we were hiking through the forest, dropping little pieces of bread along the way to mark our trail back.

Uncle Tim had drawn the green line before we got on the boat. It went way, way out in the ocean. For now our plan was to get to a shallow spot and catch some fish for lunch.

I could steer by turning the knob on the autopilot from anywhere in the boat, or I could also steer the boat by hand by turning off the autopilot and using either the big shiny wheel in the saloon or the big shiny wheel in the cockpit. Mary said they almost never steer by hand except when they dock or anchor. I could control the engine to speed up or slow down from the lever controls in the saloon or another set of levers in the cockpit. The speed control was called the throttle and another lever, called the shifter, put the engine in forward or neutral or reverse if you wanted to go forward or drift or go backward. I left it in forward. I didn't touch the throttle, either.

The chart plotter was in the cockpit, so I hadn't seen it before, but Mary showed me a second display in the saloon. I thought it was a TV. When we turned it on, we saw the green line and the red line and the pictures of the shore on the map. Mary said there was a map of the whole world in the electronics and detailed charts of the local area that showed depths and rocks to miss and shipwrecks and buoys and lighthouses and everything. Pretty cool.

Mary went back to her sewing and left me in control. I had the con.

Every half hour, I checked the engine room to see if it was on fire, and I looked around outside the boat, and I double-checked our course against our path.

"You're doing well," Mary said after two hours. "Do you need a break?"

"Nope," I said, "this is fun. But we're almost to that shallow spot. Should I get Uncle Tim?"

"He'll know," she said.

I thought for a minute. "Because we'll slow down?"

"Good job," she said. "Any change in the engine noise and your uncle will be on deck in an instant."

Twenty minutes later, with Mary standing next to me, I pulled the throttle back to slow the engine all the way down, then pulled the shifter to straight up, which was neutral. The noise level dropped to almost nothing, but I felt a bigger vibration in my feet, like something was shaking the boat. Looking outside, I saw that we were still moving but much slower than before.

"Now switch the autopilot off," Mary said.

I reached down and threw the switch.

"You can't steer the boat unless we're moving," she said.

Before I was done turning off the autopilot, Uncle Tim was in the saloon. Isaac came out of our cabin and stood at the bottom of the steps near the door to the head. He still had the book under his arm.

Uncle Tim took a quick look at the chart plotter, got a nod from Mary, and shook my hand.

"Nice job," he said. "Let's go fishing!"

Uncle Tim didn't need to yell, but I guess he was excited.

"OK, boys," he yelled. "This is lingcod fishing. They're down deep, right on the bottom. Watch me on the first one."

He flipped a lever on his fishing reel, and the line started to pay out as the big shiny metal lure dropped into the water. I'd never seen fishing gear anywhere near this big.

"Get the lure down quickly, right to the bottom"—his line went slack—"then get it off the bottom right away, before it snags on a rock." He gave his reel three quick turns. "If you feel the bottom again, reel in again. If you don't feel the bottom for a while, let the lure drop, then pick it up. You've got to be close to the bottom, but not on the bottom, to catch these monsters!"

My lure dropped smoothly, but the line on Isaac's reel got all tangled up in a big tangled ball. Once he cleared it, his line was tight.

"I've got one," he yelled, hanging on the pole with all his strength. It was bent way, way over.

"No, you don't," Uncle Tim said. "You're hooked on the bottom. Just break it off, and get a new lure."

Isaac pulled as hard as he could. The rod just bent a little more. "I think it's a fish," he yelled, "a really big fish!"

"Just break it off, then get a new lure and be more careful next time."

I felt my lure bounce off something, so I turned the reel three times.

"Good job, Jimi," Uncle Tim said. "Now wiggle the lure a little bit."

I raised and lowered the fishing rod tip just a little, then the rod tip bent over almost completely and almost tore the rod out of my hands. I had to shift my feet and lean way back to balance the pull.

"Looks like I caught the bottom, too," I said. "Should I just break it off?"

Uncle Tim looked over at me and smiled. "That's not the bottom," he said. "Just take your time, and reel it in. Keep the pressure on."

It took me a long time to get the fish to the boat. Isaac's line finally broke while I was reeling in my fish, but instead of getting another lure, he just laid the rod in the cockpit.

Uncle Tim hooked a fish, too, but he had his in the boat before mine.

Mary had the net when I got my fish up. It was longer than my arm and looked more like a snake than a fish.

"Look at those teeth!" Isaac said.

The fish's mouth was about one-fourth of its body, and lined with a million teeth like a row of little sharp nails. Also, its mouth was lime green inside. It was the weirdest fish I had ever seen.

"Great job, Jimi," Uncle Tim said, putting the fish into a big white cooler strapped to the deck at the back of the boat. "Now go back and get another one!"

"Where's your fish?" I asked. "Was yours big, too?"

Uncle Tim smiled. "No, Jimi, you got me beat. My little rockfish was nowhere near as big as your lingcod."

"You caught a rockfish?" Mary asked. She sounded surprised. "I thought it was too deep out here."

"Me, too," Uncle Tim said. "But it came up, and it's dead, so it's in the cooler."

"Bummer," Mary said. "Are you going to keep fishing?"

"We need the meat," Uncle Tim said. "You know that."

Mary shook her head and went back inside the cabin.

Uncle Tim shook his shoulders and looked at his feet. He didn't like disappointing Mary, I guess.

"You guys come here," he said, motioning with his hand toward the cooler. "You should know what we're talking about."

He opened the cooler. On the ice, next to my huge snake-looking fish, was a smaller fish that was way prettier and way more fish-looking. It was all orange and white, like it was painted for a T-shirt or something, and it had spiky fins that looked exactly like a fish would look if you were asked to draw a fish.

"This," Uncle Tim said, "is a canary rockfish. It's endangered, because it doesn't migrate and it's easy to catch, and because it has this." He pointed at a white sausage-looking thing hanging out of the fish's mouth.

"It's a swim bladder, a gas-filled bag that allows the fish to adjust its buoyancy and hang suspended in the water column at a specific depth without having to swim up or down."

He pulled a knife from his pocket and opened the blade.

"But when we catch these fish in deep water, and then quickly haul them up to the surface, the gas in the bladder gets stuck and expands and forces the swim bladder outside the fish's body."

He stuck the knife into the swim bladder, just outside the fish's mouth. It popped like a balloon.

"With a stuck swim bladder, the rockfish can't swim back down—it can't swim at all really—and it dies."

"Even if you pop it?" Isaac asked.

"Then it dies because its swim bladder won't work."

"So we're going to eat it, even though it's an endangered species?" I asked.

"It's dead anyway," Uncle Tim said. He closed the blade on his knife and put it back in his pocket. "It's not really endangered, either. It's just listed as 'threatened.' That's not as bad."

Then he closed the lid on the cooler.

"Let me move the boat, and then we'll get back to fishing!"

Uncle Tim restarted the engine and drove back to where we started fishing the first time. He said that water current and the breeze pushed us off the shallow spot.

"Come on, Isaac, get that lure back in the water!" Uncle Tim was enthusiastic again.

"No, thanks," Isaac said. "I found this to read." He held up a comic book-looking magazine.

"You'd rather read a comic book than fish?" I asked.

"It's the fishing regulations," Isaac said. "Cool stuff."

I should have left Isaac at home.

I dropped my lure just like last time but didn't hook anything. Same with Uncle Tim.

"We'll try one more drift," Uncle Tim said, "then we've got to get going."

"It says here," Isaac said, "that everyone that's fishing needs a fishing license." Isaac was sitting at the front of the cockpit and was yelling a little.

"So?" Uncle Tim said.

"Do Jimi and I have licenses?"

Uncle Tim gave Isaac a dirty look, but Isaac didn't notice. He knows when to keep his head down.

"Well," Uncle Tim said, "you're not fishing, so that's fine. I have a license. Mary has a license but she's not fishing, so we have two people fishing and two licenses. Close enough."

Isaac just kept reading.

Jimi & Isaac 2a:

Uncle Tim caught a big lingcod right away and brought it right up to the boat. His was a little smaller than mine, though. Then I hooked another one. It was a little smaller than both fish but still a good size.

"That's it for you, Jimi," Isaac yelled. "You're done."

"Now what are you talking about?" Uncle Tim asked.

"Two per person per day—that's the limit."

"Two per day per license on the boat," Uncle Tim said.

"That's not what it says in the rules," Isaac said.

Uncle Tim didn't answer.

"I don't mind," I said. "I'm kind of tired anyway."

I grabbed Isaac's fishing rod and put both his and mine away.

"Oops," Isaac said.

Uncle Tim didn't move, except his shoulders tightened up.

"Lingcod fishing season's over," Isaac said. "It was over the last day of the month."

"That's today," Uncle Tim said.

"That was yesterday," Isaac said. "Salmon season starts today. We should be salmon fishing."

Uncle Tim looked at me. I nodded.

"Crap," he said.

Uncle Tim reeled in and put his fishing rod away.

"Jimi," Uncle Tim said, "have Mary help you get moving and headed for Otter Cove. I'll get these fish cleaned and in the freezer before the fish police seize my boat."

Chapter 7:
Unintended Consequences.

"You boys should have tried the rockfish," Uncle Tim said. Then he discarded a jack of spades. I didn't need jacks.

I just shrugged. Seemed obvious to me.

"It's the best tasting fish you'll ever have—sweet and buttery and flaky," Uncle Tim said.

Mary picked up the jack and discarded a nine of spades. So she needed more jacks.

"What if that rockfish was the last one?" Isaac asked. Good point.

"It's not," Mary said. "There are plenty of them around. Just not as many as there used to be."

Isaac picked up the blind card and discarded a three of something. Nobody collects threes.

"You know why the rockfish are gone?" Uncle Tim said. "People don't think things through. It's the perfect example of unintended consequences."

"What's that mean?" I asked. Then I picked up the blind card. It was the seven of hearts, which completed my straight. One more card and I'd be out. I discarded the six of diamonds. No more collecting sixes for me.

"Well…" Uncle Tim said.

"I'm out," Isaac said. He had picked up my six and finished his hand. Three eights and a straight of four diamonds, with my six at the bottom.

"…there you go, Jimi," Uncle Tim said. "You thought getting rid of the six would help you, but instead it cost you the game. Losing was the unintended consequence."

"So the rockfish tossed a six?" Isaac said, gathering the cards. It wasn't his turn to deal, but he liked to shuffle anyway.

"Nope," Uncle Tim said, "the problem was the salmon. Around here, the salmon are like little silver gods."

"Because of the Indians," Isaac said. "They worship nature and stuff."

"No, Isaac," Mary said, "just listen for a minute."

"Not the Indians," Uncle Tim said, "because of the fishermen. Sport fishing and commercial fishing are both big, big money around here. When the salmon population collapsed a few years ago..."

"Because of overfishing," I said. "They were too greedy."

"Maybe," Uncle Tim said, "but probably not. Probably ocean conditions and dry rivers and poor hatchery management—"

"Hatchery management?" Isaac interrupted.

"—and just plain bad luck," Uncle Tim said. He looked at Isaac a little longer than usual. Isaac didn't get it.

"Many of the salmon in our waters are not natural. They're grown and raised in hatcheries like chickens, then released into the streams to grow in the wild."

"Anyway..." Mary said.

Uncle Tim looked at her and smiled. "Right. So anyway, salmon were in trouble, and the government shut down salmon fishing. The entire fishing industry had nothing to do, but they still wanted to catch fish. So they started fishing for bottom fish like lingcod and rockfish. They were pretty successful, too."

"So what?" I said. "We were fishing for lingcod today, right?"

"Right," Uncle Tim said. "When the salmon population recovered and the fishermen went back to fishing salmon, the lingcod population recovered. Big lingcod moved into our area from other places and started spawning right away. But the rockfish don't migrate; they don't move around. So once the big breeding fish are dead and gone…"

"They stay dead. Got it," Isaac said, handing the shuffled deck to Mary to deal. "Are we playing cards or what?"

"The rockfish don't come back, right," Uncle Tim said. "So by protecting the salmon, the government killed the rockfish. Now they say they're trying to protect the rockfish, but they can't without hurting the lingcod fishing industry."

"Maybe we should just eat chicken," I said.

Mary started to deal. "Maybe you're right," she said.

"No," Uncle Tim said, "we should eat fish. Fish are good for us, really healthy food. We just need to figure the whole thing out; we need to grow more fish. We need more baby fish, more food for the fish, and better growing conditions for the adult fish. It all comes down to habitat restoration. That's why we need to get the sea otters back."

Mary finished dealing and straightened her back. "Last hand," she said, "then I need to check the anchor and go to bed."

"Otters are cool," Isaac said. "I see them in the pond at home all the time."

"Those are river otters," Uncle Tim said. "Not the same at all."

"You're up, Isaac," Mary said. "Shut up and play. Everybody shut up and play."

Chapter 8:
It's Not a Swimming Pool.

"Breakfast in the cockpit, boys," Mary said, leaning down the stairs.

I was just about to get up anyway. The bacon smelled pretty good. Luckily, though, I was a little slow.

"On my way," Isaac yelled, dropping to the floor. He would have smashed into me if I'd gotten up any quicker. Isaac slept in his clothes, so he was gone as soon as he landed, but I had to put on some pants first.

Everyone was eating by the time I got up into the cockpit. It was a pretty blue-sky morning, too, and the sun was just starting to show over more huge trees on the edge of the cove.

"We saved you some bacon," Mary said, handing me a plate, "but you better be quick."

I took the two pieces left. I could see Isaac still had two in his hand and one in his mouth. Uncle Tim had four on his plate.

"Did you get any?" I asked.

"I'm fine," Mary said. "Get some pancakes, too."

I grabbed three pancakes off the stack and piled on the butter and syrup. We hardly ever get pancakes at home anymore. Mom says we might as well eat candy bars for breakfast.

Uncle Tim took a bite of his one pancake and pointed with his fork.

"You guys see that boat?" he said.

Isaac and I turned in our seats. Uncle Tim was pointing over our heads. A big silver boat was at the other end of the cove. A diver was sitting on a shelf at the back. He was wearing a black wetsuit and a mask, just like a scuba diver, but there was an orange hose running to his regulator, so he didn't have a tank on his back.

"Are they Indians?" Isaac asked.

Mary snorted in her coffee a little. You'd think she'd see it coming by now.

"They're diving for sea urchins," Uncle Tim said. "Another unintended consequence."

Uncle Tim wanted us to say "Huh?" or "Why" or something, but Isaac and I were hungry. We just went back to our pancakes.

Uncle Tim kept going anyway. Big surprise.

"The sea urchins eat the kelp," he said, "like rabbits eat the lettuce in your mom's garden. So when there's too many sea urchins, the kelp disappears, and when the kelp disappears, there's no place for the young fish to hide while they're growing up. They get eaten before they get big enough to spawn."

I knew spawning meant laying eggs and sex and stuff, but my mouth was full, so I just shrugged and made an interested face.

"They've only been harvesting sea urchins for a short time," said Uncle Tim. "Nobody eats them but the Japanese."

Uncle Tim just sat there, looking at us. I finished what was in my mouth, loaded my fork, then let him off the hook.

"Why are there too many sea urchins now?" I asked. I made the interested face again, too.

"Exactly the issue," Uncle Tim said, pointing at me with his fork and chewing on his bacon. "The only animal that eats sea urchins around here is the sea otter, and they were all killed a hundred years ago. Once the sea otters were gone, the sea urchins killed the kelp. Then the baby fish and the food fish didn't have a safe place to hide and grow, so all the other fish populations were hurt, too. The sea -otters were the key. That's why they're called a 'keystone species.' Once they were removed, the whole thing fell apart."

"Who would kill sea otters?" Isaac said, finally clearing his plate. "They don't hurt anyone."

"That was your chance, Isaac," Mary said, putting two more pancakes on Isaac's plate. "You blew it."

Uncle Tim smiled. Mary slid the last two pancakes onto my plate.

"The Indians, mostly," Uncle Tim said. "Actually the Aleuts, the Eskimos. They killed the otters and sold the pelts to the Russian and American traders. This all happened a long, long time ago. Now the only otters left are in Russia and Japan."

"That seems unlikely," Isaac said, with his mouth completely full. "Indians love nature."

"There are some otters in California and a few spots on the coast, too," Uncle Tim said, "but that's almost like a zoo situation. There used to be otters everywhere."

"Don't you have a phone call to make?" Mary said to Uncle Tim. She started collecting the empty dishes.

"That's right!" I said, also with my mouth full. I chewed and swallowed as quickly as I could. "Did you call my mom yet?"

Uncle Tim looked into his coffee cup. "Not yet," he said. "I'll get right on it."

Mary dropped the dishes into the sink.

There was a little boat hanging by some ropes at the back of the *DUCK*. While Isaac and I got the dishes done, Uncle Tim lowered it into the water and put an outboard motor on the back. Isaac and I got there just as he got the motor started.

"I'll be right back, guys," he said, yelling a little over the noise of the idling outboard. "There's no phone service here in Otter Cove, so I'll take the dinghy into shore and hike over that little hill."

"Let me come," Isaac said, with big eyes. I knew he was trying to look helpful, but he looked like an owl.

Uncle Tim frowned and reached back for the motor controls, but Mary was cool.

"Go get your life jacket on," she said. "Hurry up."

"I don't need it," Isaac said, making a big smile. "I can swim really well."

Mary looked at him all seriously, then cracked a big smile and put a hand on his shoulder. "Are you sure," she said, "that you'll be safe?"

"Absolutely," Isaac said, standing up as tall as he could. "I'm a great swimmer!"

Mary looked at Uncle Tim, who shrugged his shoulders.

"OK, then," she said, "just be careful!"

Isaac raised his foot onto the front of the dinghy. I'm pretty sure Mary let go of the rope holding the dinghy at the same time she gave Isaac a little push. Maybe not, but I'm pretty sure.

Isaac twisted in the air for just a moment, made a grab for Mary, and then splashed into the water. Uncle Tim nodded at Mary, gunned the motor, and took off for shore.

Jimi & Isaac 2a:

When Isaac came back to the surface, he was a mess. He was trying to yell, but no noise came out. He was trying to swim, but all he did was flap his arms around.

Mary looked at me and pointed. I followed her pointing and saw an aluminum pole lying on the deck. I grabbed it and handed it to her.

She grabbed one end of the pole with her right hand, and the rail of the boat with her left hand. Then she hit Isaac in the arm with the other end of the pole, pretty hard.

"Grab this," she said.

Isaac's eyes were huge. He just looked at her.

"Grab it!" she yelled, and hit him in the arm again.

Isaac grabbed the pole and tried to pull it and Mary into the water. She pulled back and dragged Isaac over to the little ladder on the back of the boat. Finally Isaac grabbed the ladder.

"It's pretty cold, huh?" she said.

Isaac nodded, then climbed up the ladder.

"Isaac, get your clothes off," she said. "I'll go in the boat and give you boys some privacy. Jimi, hose him off before he goes below. I don't want any salt water or wet clothes belowdecks."

I nodded. She looked at Isaac. He was shivering too hard to nod.

She grabbed his hair and got right in his face. "You need to wear a life jacket! The ocean is not a swimming pool! Got it?"

Isaac looked at her and shivered. His arms were starting to flap around. He looked like his muscles were completely out of control.

"Get his clothes rinsed out and hang them in the cockpit to dry, too," she said to me. "We'll get under way as soon as your uncle gets back."

Then she turned away and went below. Isaac was lying on the deck, already undressed. The hose water was cold, too.

Chapter 9:
Get Serious.

It was pretty quiet for a while.

Finally I saw Uncle Tim, on shore, getting back into the dinghy.

I guess Mary saw him too, because she came out of her cabin.

"Put your life jacket on," she said, "and come with me. Time to learn about the anchor." She was on deck before I could answer. I guess it wasn't a question.

She waited for me at the front of the boat. Actually, she almost waited for me. She started talking almost as soon as I got on deck.

"If the engine quits," she said, "you don't die for a while. You drift, and you call for help on the radio, and if the radio works and somebody hears you, then probably somebody helps you."

Made sense, I guess, even though Uncle Tim said the engine would run forever. I guess Mary didn't buy it either.

"But if your anchor doesn't hold, or the chain fails, or if you don't set the anchor correctly," she said, "you can drift ashore, break up on the rocks, and die in your sleep."

I was finally up at the front with her. "The pointy end," she called it. The boat name for it is the "bow," which is pronounced like "cow," not like "slow."

"You need to know how to handle the anchor by yourself," she said. "If your uncle falls down and hits his head, you'll need to take over."

"Isaac can probably figure it out," I said. "He's pretty smart."

She just looked at me. I think she was deciding if she should push me in the water.

"I'll learn it," I said.

"Good," she said.

She showed me the anchor chain and the electric winch that hauls the chain back on board, and the switches that control the winch.

"This winch is extremely powerful," she said. "It will tear your arms off if your jacket gets caught in the chain."

Jimi & Isaac 2a:

She showed me where to stand to run the switches and where to stand to work with the chain.

"Keep your hands away from the chain while you use the winch," she said, three times in three different ways.

Uncle Tim was at the back of the boat and had the outboard off the dinghy and the dinghy back hanging from the ropes. Mary gave him a thumbs-up. He started the boat and moved forward a little.

"The winch is super powerful," Mary said, "but you still don't want to use it to drag the boat around. Your uncle will drive the boat over the anchor, and then we'll lift it and the chain off the bottom."

There was a lot of chain out. It took a long time to winch it back in. Mary let me run the switch.

"If it's calm like this," Mary said, "we put out one hundred feet of chain in twenty feet of water. If it's thirty feet deep, we put out one hundred and fifty feet of chain."

"So five times the depth," I said.

"Right." She looked a little surprised. Maybe she thought I couldn't do math.

"If it's windy or there's waves, we use at least seven to one," she said. "In a storm, we'll put out even more. The flatter we pull on the anchor, the better it holds."

Finally the chain was completely vertical. The winch got a little louder and slower, then quieter and faster again.

"The anchor was really stuck," Mary said. "That's good." She turned to Uncle Tim and made a stirring motion with her finger. He gave her the OK signal.

I leaned over the railing and saw the anchor coming up through the water.

"Stop at the surface," Mary said. "Then bring it up slow."

We got the anchor all on deck and "secured," which means tied off with a rope.

Mary gave Uncle Tim the stirring signal again. He put the *DUCK* in gear and pushed the throttle forward, and we were back at sea in no time.

Isaac finally came out of our cabin. He found a book on sea otters and wedged himself into a seat in the corner of the saloon. I had the con for most of the day. Mary did some more stitching, and Uncle Tim hid in his cabin some more.

"Mary," I said, "are you getting off the boat here?"

I pointed to a harbor on the chart plotter where our course took a sharp turn.

She looked over the top of her stitching.

"Yep," she said. "That's as far as I go."

"Well," I said, "we'll be there in two hours, and it seems like Isaac should learn to run the boat too."

"Yep," she said. "That's a good idea, Jimi."

Then she went back to her stitching.

"Will you show him what to do?" I asked. That seemed like the best plan.

She looked over the top of her stitching.

"Nope," she said.

"But Uncle Tim is still in his cabin," I said.

She just looked at me for a while.

"You show him," she said finally. "I'll listen in. You'll do fine."

Isaac didn't want to put down his book, but Mary glanced at him over her sewing and he changed his mind. I showed him the autopilot and the steering wheels and the throttles and the shifters, and how to look around inside the boat and look around outside the boat.

"Is that everything?" I asked Mary.

Mary put down her sewing. She smiled at me, then turned her face to Isaac.

"Isaac," she said, "look at me."

Isaac was playing with the autopilot controls, but he put them in his lap and looked at her. Right in the eyes, too. I was impressed.

"What does it mean, Isaac," she said, "if you have the con?"

"The controls," he answered, right away, "it means that I have the controls."

"Good answer," she said, "but not the whole answer."

She waited.

"She means—" I said, but Mary held up her hand.

"Let him," she said.

Isaac moved his jaw and looked out the window. Rats. He was gone, thinking about something else.

"It means I'm responsible for the boat," he said, turning back to Mary.

"Right," she said. "Whatever happens, you're responsible. On the boat, to the boat, around the boat. It's up to you to fix it or get it fixed."

"Got it," he said. He gave her a thumbs-up, too, and smiled a little.

She smiled, too, just a little, and went back to her sewing.

We pulled into the harbor where Mary was going to get off the *DUCK*. I hadn't noticed it on the chart, but the harbor was right in the middle of a town. Stores and streets and a big building with windows right above where we were dropping the anchor. Uncle Tim helped Isaac handle the boat from the helm while I set the anchor at the bow. Uncle Tim and Mary didn't have to do anything except watch and tell us what to do a few times. It was like Isaac and I knew what we were doing.

Isaac and I kept our life jackets on for the dinghy ride in. Then we had to carry them around, because Uncle Tim figured they'd get stolen if we left them in the dinghy. Isaac wore his, so he looked like an idiot. I carried mine, so I looked like an idiot, too, I suppose. Uncle Tim and Mary didn't wear life jackets in the dinghy. Their two really ragged ones were stuffed under the seat. I guess when you're an adult having life jackets around is as good as having life jackets on.

We stopped off at the bus station to check the schedule.

"Three hours," Uncle Tim said. "Let's eat!"

That got Isaac's attention.

There was a huge restaurant on a pier right above where we tied off the dinghy. From our table we could see the dinghy, and the *DUCK* at anchor in the harbor, and the ocean forever in every direction.

We were early for dinner, and there was a special early-bird menu. The restaurant was full of old people. I liked it. Less fancy, more friendly.

Isaac and I both had crab cakes for appetizers and salmon steaks with rice for the meal. Uncle Tim and Mary shared a salad full of crab and salmon and mussels, which are little black clams.

There was really good bread, and you could have as much as you wanted. Isaac and I wanted a lot. After a while they got slower about bringing us more. I guess you could have as much bread as you could get them to bring you.

After dinner, we sat on the shore below the restaurant. Before too long, Isaac, Uncle Tim and I were all throwing rocks into the water. Uncle Tim somehow found some flat rocks that he could skip. Isaac just kept looking for bigger and bigger rocks to throw. Finally he tried to throw a huge boulder the size of his head. He slipped, and it dropped at his feet. The splash got his pants all wet. It looked like he peed himself.

Mary just sat a little ways up the shore, hugging her knees.

"Do you want me to bring you some rocks?" I asked.

"No, Jimi," she said, "but thank you. You boys throw your rocks, make your splashes. I'll watch."

It seemed like she had something else to say, so I waited.

"It looks like that's the way it works," she said.

Uncle Tim gave Isaac and me a little money and sent us to the grocery store while he took Mary to the bus station. We got some potato chips and some chocolate cookies. Hardly anybody stared at Isaac's pants.

We had our life jackets on and the dinghy all ready when Uncle Tim finally showed up. Isaac started the outboard and drove to the *DUCK*.

Chapter 10:
Big Ocean.

The next morning, I got the anchor aboard and stowed. Soon after we left the harbor, we couldn't see the town or the beach, just the trees on the hills behind the town. Pretty soon after that, we couldn't see individual trees, just green, and right after that, the fog covered the trees and the mountains behind them. We still had blue skies overhead and the ocean was blue, but there was a foggy white wall all around the boat.

"It's misty here, too," Uncle Tim said, "but it's so thin you don't see it. It's only when you look through miles of it sideways that it looks white."

"Besides," he said, "you can't see as far as you think. If the ocean is completely calm, and your eyes are six feet above the water, the horizon is only six miles away."

That was crazy talk.

"Because it's curved?" Isaac asked.

"Right," said Uncle Tim. "The earth curves way more than people think. Of course Columbus and all those early sailors knew the earth was round. Any thinking person that's been on the ocean knows it's not flat."

"They thought it was turtles…" Isaac said.

Uncle Tim just shook his head.

"…all the way down."

Isaac was shaking, he was laughing so hard. I'd heard the turtle thing before, but it still didn't make any sense, and it still wasn't funny.

"Let's go fishing," Uncle Tim said. "Real fishing. Salmon fishing."

"That's a good idea," Isaac said. "Salmon season is open now. Two per day per person. But Jimi and I still don't have licenses."

"Isaac," Uncle Tim got real tall, "I'm going salmon fishing. I'm going to catch salmon, clean salmon, and put salmon in the freezer. I need the fish."

Isaac just looked at him.

"If you don't want to fish," he continued, "that's fine. If Jimi doesn't want to fish"—he waved at me, or toward me—"that's fine, too. But I don't want to hear another word about the fishing regulations, got it?"

Isaac shrugged. He gathered the book on otters and curled up in his corner of the saloon.

Uncle Tim took out the fishing rods we used for lingcod and changed out the shiny heavy lures for little pink plastic tassels with huge hooks.

"Hootchies," he said, holding one up. "The simple ideas are usually the best."

He put a rod in a holder on each side of the boat and let the lures back until we could barely see the hootchies dive underwater and then skid on top.

"Jimi," he said, "why don't you just drive the boat and let me handle the fishing?"

"Sure," I said. "That sounds like a good plan. I like to drive."

"Just do me a favor," Uncle Tim said, "let me know if you see any boats headed our way."

"No problem," I said, "except for the fog."

"That's why," he said, pressing some buttons on the chart plotter, "we have radar."

The radar on the *DUCK* wasn't like the radar I'd seen in movies where there was a big round green screen and a moving line like a pie slice and knobs and dials everywhere. This radar just put orange on the screen where it saw something.

So now we had an orange line right at the same place where the electronic chart showed the shore should be, because the radar saw the beach. All the buoys really showed up, too.

"They're specially designed," Uncle Tim said, "to reflect the radar signal. A tiny buoy or shore marker looks like a huge ship on the radar."

Then he showed me an ocean freighter thirteen miles away. The orange mark was pretty big, and we could watch it move toward us.

"How come we can see it on radar," I asked, "if it's more than six miles away? Can the radar see over the curvature?"

Uncle Tim just pointed up.

I followed his finger. Halfway up the mast was a round plastic box.

"That's the radar antenna," he said. "It's higher up so it sees farther."

I thought for a moment and drew the picture in my mind. Then I thought of something.

"If we're looking at something tall, we can see it farther away, too," I said.

"Absolutely," Uncle Tim said, "and it's a simple thing. The horizon is six miles away when your eye is six feet up, so you can see something six feet tall twelve miles away."

"Cool," I said.

"Of course it's not that simple," Uncle Tim said. "Air layers near the water bend light and create mirages, just like in the desert. You'll even see tunnels where you can see land with water below and water above. It can get pretty weird out here."

I had to agree with that. It had been pretty weird so far.

"Now," Uncle Tim said, "for fishing. See that line in the water?"

Ahead and to the right, I could easily see what he was talking about. The water on our side of the line was blue-green. It was almost black on the other side. The line curved away as far as I could see in both directions.

"That's a tide rip," Uncle Tim said. "Water coming in from the ocean on one side, water coming out from the bay on the other side. The fish will follow that rip, looking for food on one side or the other. We'll follow it too, looking for fish. Just don't get too close to the rip itself. There will be trees and branches and garbage and weeds and all kinds of debris trapped in it."

"Cool," I said.

"You'll probably have to hand-steer," Uncle Tim said, "and keep a good lookout. We may even need to get His Highness on deck."

"I'll manage," I said.

Chapter 11:
Big Water. Big Fish.

"Fish on!" Uncle Tim yelled. "Put it in neutral, Jimi!"

I dropped the throttle to idle and moved the shifter to neutral. The boat slowed, but I could still steer as long as we coasted through the water. If we got too slow, I would put the engine in gear for just a moment so I could keep the *DUCK* pointed the right way.

Uncle Tim grabbed the fishing rod and yanked the tip up. "Setting the hook," he called it. The idea was to pull extra hard on the fishing line so the point of the hook went all the way through the salmon's lip and didn't fall out later.

"This is a big salmon," Uncle Tim said. "Stay by the controls, and keep the stern pointed at the fish so we don't get tangled up."

I hadn't seen the fish, but his fishing pole was bending farther than it did with the other three fish Uncle Tim already had in the freezer. He just reeled those to the boat and lifted them aboard. He couldn't even reel this one in.

"She'll come," he said, "as soon as she gets tired. While they're running fast, they don't have any water passing through their gills. Their blood runs out of oxygen pretty quickly."

The fish stopped pulling right after that. Uncle Tim reeled as fast as he could.

"I need to get her in the boat before she recovers," he said. "If I let her rest, we'll have to start again."

He didn't reel fast enough, I guess. As soon as the fish came close to the boat and Uncle Tim reached for the net, the fish took off. Uncle Tim almost dropped his fishing pole.

"Turn Jimi!" he yelled, "Keep the stern pointed at the fish!"

I looked at the direction his rod was pointing. Then I put the boat into forward gear and gave it a little throttle while I spun the wheel. Once the boat swung around, I cut the throttle, put it back in neutral, and centered the rudder.

"Great job, Jimi," Uncle Tim yelled. "We'll get her yet!"

The fish took three more runs before we finally got it in the boat. It was way, way bigger than the other fish.

"Forty pounds, maybe!" Uncle Tim said, standing straight and bending his back backward. "Meat!"

He wrapped his hand around the fish's tail. Only the fin stuck out the top of his hand.

"Don't wanna drop this one," he said, smiling.

He grabbed a long, thin knife from a sheath he'd tied to the rail and held the fish over the water. Just like he'd done with the smaller fish, he slit the belly from tail to head, then made another cut across the fish, just behind the head. All the guts dropped into the ocean with a big *bloop*.

He slid the knife back into its sheath and turned to me, still holding the fish over the water.

"We'll let her bleed for a while," he said. "It makes the meat taste better."

Soon the blood stopped running, then the drips got smaller. Uncle Tim took the fish down below and was quickly back on deck.

"One more," he said, "then we'll call it a day. We'll call it a pretty good day."

Uncle Tim reset the fishing gear and we started fishing again, but we'd moved off the tide rip. Now we couldn't find it again. It was like it disappeared.

"Oh, well," Uncle Tim said after thirty minutes of looking, "let's get under way. We've got some miles to cover in the next twenty-four hours."

Chapter 12:
Covering the Miles.

After Uncle Tim got the fishing gear put away, he went below for a few minutes. When he came back on deck, he was all cleaned up. He even had changed his shirt.

"I'll take the con," he said. "You go take a nap. Tell Isaac to take one, too. You guys have the evening watch tonight, so you'll need to be alert."

Isaac was already asleep in the saloon. The book on otters was on the counter next to him. I went downstairs to my bunk. I don't remember lying down.

"Soup's on! Hot soup!" Isaac was yelling from the saloon.

"Come and get it! Hot Soup! Supply is limited! Act now!"

"Isaac," I heard Uncle Tim say, "shut up."

I guess nap time was over. Time for dinner.

We each had a big bowl of canned soup, but it was the good kind of canned soup with lots of ingredients, not the cheap kind of canned soup my mom fixes for lunch when she can't figure out what to fix for lunch.

"I'll get the dishes," Uncle Tim said, picking up the bowls and taking them to the sink. "You guys take a look around the boat. You'll share the first watch tonight. Look out for each other. I'll get up at midnight and go until morning."

Isaac and Uncle Tim went through the engine room together. They checked the oil and coolant levels, and all the temperatures and the fuel filters.

"I'll check all that again at midnight," Uncle Tim said. "Don't go in the engine room while I'm asleep. Just open the hatch every hour and look around. Wake me if you see anything that needs attention."

"What if we run out of gas?" Isaac asked.

"There's no gas on this boat," Uncle Tim said. "Our engine runs on diesel fuel. We use a little under a gallon per hour, so we should have"—his eyes rolled back and shut as he looked inside his forehead—"just over thirty hours' more fuel on this tank. We'll change tanks before then so we don't accidentally run the engine dry."

"Can we eat some more?" Isaac asked.

"Eat and drink whatever you want, but remember I'll be up at midnight, and you'll want to go straight to sleep after that, so don't eat anything weird too late in the evening."

"And life jackets on deck, right?" I said to Uncle Tim, but really to Isaac.

"Of course." Isaac said. "Duh."

Well, at least we wouldn't have to argue about it later.

"That's right," Uncle Tim said. "Put them on down here before you leave the saloon. But don't go past the cockpit after dark, and only go into the cockpit if you're both up there. Anybody that falls off the boat in the dark is pretty much dead. We'd never find them."

"Buddy system," I said.

Isaac looked at me. "Are you my buddy, Jimi?"

"I'm your buddy, Isaac."

Uncle Tim took one more look at the controls and the instruments and the chart plotter.

"All good," he said. "I'm gone."

"Good night, Uncle Tim," I said.

"Good night, Captain," Isaac said. Then he saluted.

"Jimi," Uncle Tim said, "you have the con. See you at midnight. Wake me up if I'm not up already."

Then he ducked into his cabin, leaving me in control.

Isaac grabbed another book off the bookshelf and curled up in his corner.

I went through the hourly checklist, just to get a good start, except I didn't go into the engine room. I just opened the hatch and looked around, like Uncle Tim said.

Everything was perfect. I liked having the con.

Chapter 13:
Watch.

"Isaac, what time is it?"

"Time for Jimi to buy a watch," Isaac said.

"Come on, Isaac," I said.

"There's a clock on the chart plotter. Maybe the guy on watch should look at the chart plotter every once in a while."

That was a good point. I pressed the MENU button and the CHART button to change the display. 20:27, it said. The sun was just starting to get low in the sky off to our left a little. That was a lucky thing, because I could still see the water clearly straight ahead. If I need to turn left or if the sun was slightly more to my right, I

would be heading too close to the sun to see clearly.
Then I would have to decide if I should stay on the
course and not be able to see well, or if I should turn
slightly off-course and be able to see.

Now it was 20:29.

"Isaac," I said, "why don't you take the con?"

Isaac looked over the top of his book.

"How about," he said, "you keep the con until nine,
then I'll take it for two hours, then we'll buddy-system
on watch from eleven until midnight so we don't fall
asleep."

"I don't want to wait that long," I said.

He didn't even put his book down. "It's only a half
hour."

Nine plus twelve is twenty-one, so...

"OK," I said. "Watch change at twenty-one hundred
hours."

"Aye, aye, skipper," Isaac said. He still had his face
behind the book. There was a sailboat on the cover. It
was a blue sailboat with yellow sails. Maybe sand
colored, like a brown with a little yellow. *Open Ocean
Sailing* was the title. Like you could sail on a closed
ocean.

20:32.

I clicked the knob on the autopilot and changed
course one degree right. We were pointed almost west,
so right was north. I wanted to be able to see in front of
us, and the sun was in my eyes a little.

"It's almost dark," I said.

Isaac didn't answer. He didn't even move his head.

"It will be weird driving in the dark," I said.

Isaac didn't even move an eyebrow.

"I hope we don't run into a dragon," I said.

Nothing.

"There're probably sea snakes."

Still nothing.

"Kraken, I'm guessing. Whole kraken families with kraken babies and kraken grandmothers and crazy kraken cousins with bad teeth."

Nothing.

20:38.

I zoomed out on the chart plotter until I could see all of Washington State on the map to our left, which was south, and Canada to our right, which was north. The part of Canada on the chart was a huge island that went almost to Alaska. I don't know why Canada would want such a big island. It's probably a lot of trouble to have an island that big. Maybe they would give it to me. I'd call it Jimiland. Jimiville. Jimisle. The Canadians probably wouldn't give it away, though. I'd have to buy it. So I'll need a job first so I can get rich. I'm pretty good on the guitar, so I'll just be a rock star. They're rich. My dad could be a rock star. He's better than most guitar players on the radio. He says it's not very fun to be a rock star, though, because you have to live in hotels and eat restaurant food. That doesn't sound so bad to me.

20:39.

I listened to the engine for a while. It sounded like an engine. Mechanical noises like little tiny hammers and wind noises like little tiny winds, and another noise like sliding a chair across the floor really fast, over and over.

Then I heard a Jimi Hendrix guitar riff. It wasn't really up front or clear; it was way back in the mix, but I could hear it.

"Tomorrow, or just the end of time…"

Wow.

Of course the engine wasn't playing Jimi Hendrix. That would be weird.

But still.

"Duh duh duh, duh duh duh, Help me!"

It wasn't exactly right, though. Something was missing.

"Purple Haze, all in my brain…"

Jimi Hendrix saw sounds as colors. When he heard something, it drew a picture in his head. It's a pretty common condition with wildly artistic musicians.

When I hear guitar music, I don't see colors. Mostly I see my dad playing the music. Sometimes I can feel my hands playing the riff, though.

"Is it tomorrow, or just the end of time…"

That one was really clear.

"Is it tomorrow, or just the end of time…"

"Is it tomorrow, or just the end of time…"

"Is it tomorrow, or just the end of time…"

"Tag."

That didn't sound like Jimi.

Jimi & Isaac 2a:

My eyes started working again. Isaac was standing next to me.

"Tag," he said. "I have the con."

I looked at the chart plotter.

21:02.

Cool. I handed Isaac the autopilot controls.

Chapter 14:
Some Odd Thing.

Uncle Tim's alarm clock went off at 23:50. It didn't take him long to get out of bed.

"Great job, guys," he said, taking a look at the chart plotter. "Let me get some coffee made and wash up a little, then you guys can go to bed."

Isaac went to bed anyway. "Jimi's got it," he said, going down the stairs. Uncle Tim laughed as he went back into his cabin.

"Uncle Tim," I said when he came back into the saloon.

Jimi & Isaac 2a:

"Just a second, Jimi," he said. "Let me do the engine room checks, then I'll take over."

I nodded. and he disappeared down the hatch. The motor sure was louder with the hatch open.

I double-checked all the controls and the chart plotter and autopilot settings. I wanted to make everything normal for Uncle Tim. Isaac had changed the color on the radar display to bright green, but I changed it back to orange.

The engine noise got quieter as Uncle Tim stood in the hatch, then louder as he climbed out, then really quiet when he closed the hatch.

"All is well," he said. "We'll switch fuel tanks tomorrow right before you boys go on watch."

Nothing to worry about, then. Good.

"Uncle Tim," I said.

He turned off the burner and poured himself some coffee. He left the mug on the counter and came over to where I was sitting.

"What's up?" he said. "Problems with Isaac?"

I guess I looked worried.

"No," I said, "nothing like that."

He just waited.

"I heard music."

Uncle Tim scrunched his eyebrows, then relaxed and smiled.

"In the engine?"

"Yeah."

"Cool. Your dad playing?"

"No," I said, "Jimi. The other Jimi."

"Got it," he said. "That's pretty cool. Usually I hear folk music, sometimes I hear bagpipes, but sometimes I hear rock. Jimi would be good company."

"So it's not weird?" I said.

Uncle Tim leaned back against the counter.

"It can get weird," he said. "Sometimes I hear voices talking from the back cabin or on deck. They can be as real as a family dinner. Usually, though, I can't understand the words."

"But it's not weird?"

"It's just your brain trying to make sense of the noise," he said. "Your mind will try to find patterns, even if they aren't there. It hears the engine and the wind and the water and the dishes rattling in the cabinets and your breathing and it tries to make sense of the noise. It tries to find the pattern. In your case, it turns it into music."

"It sounds weird," I said.

"The weird part," he said, "is that some people don't find patterns in the world. They don't notice that things happen together. They don't notice that you get wet when it rains."

"Maybe they don't need for everything to mean something."

"I don't want to have a brain that quiet," he said. "Everything has meaning. We just need to figure it all out. There's plenty of time to be quiet when you're dead."

Jimi & Isaac 2a:

Suddenly I was pretty tired. I think Uncle Tim saw it.

"Go to bed," he said. "I'll wake you in five hours so you can see the sun come up. No land in sight, open ocean everywhere. It's pretty spectacular. I don't want you boys to miss it. Tomorrow is going to be epic!"

Open ocean again. Like it was ever closed.

"Good night," I said.

"Good night, Jimi. We'll do some fishing tomorrow, too. You'll be surprised at what we catch out here."

The bright sunlight was shining in the deck hatch when I woke. The motor was running, just like always.

"Hey, Isaac!" I said, kicking the bottom of his bunk.

"Yeah?" he mumbled.

"Looks like Uncle Tim decided to let us sleep."

"Yeah."

"Let's get up," I said. "He'll need a break."

"Yeah."

I got out of bed and put my pants on. I took a sniff and figured my shirt would last one more day.

"You cooking oatmeal?"

"Sure," Isaac said, rolling onto his elbow.

I went up the stairs, into the saloon. Uncle Tim wasn't there. I opened the hatch into the noisy engine room and had a look around. Everything looked good but no Uncle Tim.

Isaac came up into the saloon and filled the kettle with water, then put it on the stove and lit the burner.

"Uncle Tim must be in the head," I said, and found the autopilot control on the dinette seat.

Isaac climbed partway out the companionway and looked around.

"He's not on deck," he said, returning to the cooktop and putting instant oatmeal into three coffee mugs.

I looked at the chart plotter. Several hours ago, Uncle Tim had turned right. Our path was way off of our planned course.

Isaac was on his second mug of oatmeal before I started to worry. I'd finished mine but didn't want to get another one before Uncle Tim had his. That would be a little rude.

Finally I knocked on the door to his cabin. He didn't answer, so I knocked again, loudly, and opened the door. It didn't take long to look around.

Uncle Tim was gone!

Chapter 15:
Keep Driving the Boat.

Isaac didn't even blink.

"I'll put out a Mayday!" he said.

"What's that?"

"A radio call for help. Mayday is the most serious kind of radio call."

He grabbed the book about fixing the engine and turned to the back. "The last chapter is emergency procedures," he said.

He laid the book open on the dinette table and showed me the checklist.

"First," he said, "we put on our life jackets."

Then he looked at me.

I shrugged my shoulders.

"Get the life jackets, Jimi! This is an emergency, and we need to follow these procedures!"

I didn't plan on going on deck any time soon, but Isaac was all wound up. It's completely useless to argue with wound-up Isaac. I handed him his life jacket and put mine on.

"Item one," he said, "keep driving the boat."

"What does that mean?"

He read a little. "It means that one of us should keep driving the boat, be on watch, I guess, while the other one does all the special emergency stuff. That's the best way to keep the problem from getting worse."

I shrugged my shoulders again. My uncle wasn't on the boat. What part of that didn't Isaac understand? It wasn't going to get worse. Losing your uncle is worse than anything.

"Item two is to put out a Mayday call," he said. "You drive, Jimi; I'll do the emergency stuff."

Whatever. I guess he had the book.

"Whatever," I said. "OK, I'll drive." Uncle Tim was probably dead anyway. He had said that if you fall overboard at night, nobody will find you. Isaac almost died from being in the water for thirty seconds.

Isaac started fiddling with the radio and looking at his book.

"I don't think it works," I said.

He ignored me. My uncle was dead, and my friend was reading a book.

Jimi & Isaac 2a:

"Mary said the radio didn't work!" I said. "She said she's been telling Uncle Tim to fix it for a month."

She won't have to tell him anymore, I thought, *because he's dead.*

"Mayday, Mayday, Mayday," Isaac yelled into the microphone. "This is the vessel *DUCK*."

He checked the book.

"We are at…" He stopped and fiddled with the chart plotter, and then shouted our position into the microphone. "Our captain is lost overboard! We need help!"

Well, he got that part right.

Isaac did the whole Mayday thing again, all the way through.

Then he read a little farther down the list.

"We need to start a search," he said. "We can do a grid pattern or a circle pattern."

"You're an idiot," I said. "Where are we going to search?"

That stumped him. He just looked at me and opened and closed his mouth. Three times. My uncle was dead, and my friend thought he was a fish. Great.

"Wait!" I said. "Mary told me!"

"Told you what?" Isaac said. "Mary said a lot."

"The chart plotter," I said. "It makes two lines. Our course line, that we're way off, and our path—the red line. Mary called it bread crumbs."

"Feed the birds, then," Isaac said. "What's your point?"

"We need to follow the bread crumbs back to Uncle Tim."

"Good call, Jimi." Isaac said. "I think you're right. But we need to drive outside. We can't see good enough from down here."

He was right. I turned the boat around while he got our coats. We took off our life jackets, put our coats on, then put our life jackets back on. Then we went into the cockpit.

We needed to find Uncle Tim.

Maybe he wasn't dead.

Chapter 16:
Trouble Cascade.

I turned the boat around and drove back on our path. I tried to drive exactly on the path, as close as I could. Isaac went to the front of the cockpit and looked for Uncle Tim. He did a good job, too. His head went back and forth, back and forth.

"I'm trying to look everywhere," he said. "But I don't think it works very well. I keep seeing things close to the boat that I didn't see far away, and I see stuff and then don't see it again."

"Just keep trying," I said. "You're doing fine."

I was trying to look, too, but mostly I was trying to keep the *DUCK* on our path out. It wasn't easy. I had to adjust the autopilot a lot more than I did yesterday. I didn't know if I should be looking more or driving more or doing something else to try and find Uncle Tim.

Isaac's job was hard, too. We were headed almost straight into the sun. The water was bright and sparkling and trying to kill Uncle Tim. I wanted to turn to the north or the south, so we could see where we were going, but we needed to see where we were going without turning.

Isaac was shading his eyes with his hand and doing his best, I think.

"Wait a sec," he yelled, and dropped down the companionway.

I put the *DUCK* in neutral and tried to keep it straight as it slowed down. I didn't want to move the boat without a lookout.

"Here you go," he said, climbing back on deck and handing me Mary's sunglasses. They were the stupid big round ones. Isaac was already wearing Uncle Tim's glasses. They were swoopy and cool looking. I didn't care. I wanted Isaac to wear the best glasses. I put Mary's glasses on.

"Back to the search," Isaac said. His head started moving, left to right, right to left.

"Jimi, what are you doing?" Isaac yelled.

We'd followed our path all the way back to where it turned, during the night.

"The path turns here," I said, pointing at the chart plotter. "We need to follow the path."

Isaac thought for a minute.

"Good," he said.

I did a real good job with the turn, and the *DUCK* stayed right on the path. The new track was right on top of the old track, and right on top of our old course. I was getting to be pretty good at driving my dead uncle's boat. Yay for me.

"Wait a minute!" I said, dropping the throttle to slow and taking the boat out of gear. "Isaac, come here!"

Isaac took one last big look around, then came back to where I was driving.

I pointed at the chart plotter.

"The path turns here, there." I pointed to the chart plotter and then to the water behind us.

"So?"

"So the boat didn't turn itself," I said. "Uncle Tim turned it, right here! He fell off somewhere between here and where we woke up this morning, here."

I pointed at the end of the path, where we turned around this morning.

"You're right," he said finally. "Let me make another Mayday call, and then we'll check it again. The sun is straight overhead, and we'll see better this time!"

I did less driving and more looking, too. I figured it was more important to do superdetailed looking than superaccurate driving. I also sped up a little. More speed, find him faster, better chances on the not-freezing-to-death part.

But we were soon at the end of the track.

"We'll turn around," I said, "and try again."

What else could we do?

"I'm sorry, Jimi," Isaac said. "I just can't see very far."

I looked at Isaac. Maybe he was onto something.

"You need to climb the mast!" I said. "The higher you are, the farther you can see!"

"Yeah," Isaac said, "there's a whole chapter on mast climbing in the book. I'll go get it."

The book was full of pictures of ropes and harnesses and winches and safety gear and pages and pages of stuff we didn't have.

Instead I went to the cockpit. The mast was in front of the cockpit, on the roof of the saloon. It was smooth and metal and went straight up for a long, long ways. I didn't think Isaac could climb it.

Lower down, though, there was a bunch of equipment bolted to the mast.

"Isaac," I said. "You don't need to climb all the way. If you're twice as high off the water you can see twice as far. Just stand on top of that stuff and hold on to the mast."

Isaac followed my finger to where I was pointing and nodded. "Yep," he said.

I put the *DUCK* in gear and turned around. I just took a minute to get back on our path.

Jimi & Isaac 2a:

"I might need to trade," Isaac said. "This really hurts my feet."

He made sense. Once I had to stand on a ladder for almost an hour helping Dad paint the house. That hurt my feet, too. Isaac's perch was worse than a ladder.

"Sounds good," I said. "Let me…"

Then the *DUCK* started screaming at us. It sounded like one of those car alarms that goes off all the time in parking lots, but it was much, much louder. I cut the throttle, put the gear in neutral, shut the motor off, and dove into the companionway.

Isaac was right behind me.

The saloon was full of noise. It hurt. Isaac and I were just running around, look at everything: under the seats, in the cabinets, down in the cabins, everywhere.

Finally Isaac grabbed me and pointed. Right under the radio that probably didn't work was a flashing red light. The label underneath it said: "BILGE ALARM".

Isaac grabbed his book, took a quick look at the index, and turned to a page in the middle. He read for a few seconds, then looked at me. He didn't look good.

"We're sinking!" he yelled. "We're going to die, too!"

Chapter 17:
Work the Problem.

Isaac grabbed his book, looked at the index, and read straight through the first page and the next page of the article.

"The bilge is the bottom of the boat!" he yelled, right in my ear. I could still barely hear him.

"There's water in the bilge, that's why the alarm is going off. The boat is leaking! We need to find the leak and stop it!"

He read a little bit more.

"We need to check the heads and the sink drains," he yelled. "Anywhere there's a hose or connection through the bottom of the boat. Look for leaks!"

Jimi & Isaac 2a:

I went forward and looked under the sink in the head. There were a bunch of bottles and cleaning supplies in there, but I could follow the line down from the sink drain and from the head. Both were dry. I pulled out the cleaning supplies and checked the inside of the hull, where the hoses connected to some metal pieces in the hull. It was dry. I went back to the saloon.

"No water there!" I yelled to Isaac.

"It wasn't the other head, either," he yelled. "Check the sink here!"

I checked under the saloon sink. It was dry there, too.

Isaac checked the book again.

"It must be the engine room!" he yelled.

Great. I hate the engine room. On the other hand, the alarm was starting to bother me, too. Maybe it was quieter in the engine room.

Isaac opened the hatch and dropped in. I was right behind him.

I almost crushed him. He hadn't moved out of the way. Once I stopped falling over, I could see why. His feet, and now my feet, were underwater.

We panicked. I mean, we didn't do any yelling or make faces or wave our arms and hands, but we panicked. We froze.

Then we looked at each other.

Isaac looked horrible. His eyes were way too big. He grabbed my arm right above the elbow. I realized it should have hurt, probably a lot, but I didn't feel it. We didn't move.

But after just a moment, Isaac gave my arm a double squeeze.

I looked at him, but he wasn't looking at me. I followed his eyes.

"It's going down!" he yelled.

"I got it," I yelled. "I understand! We're sinking!"

"No!" he yelled back. "It's going down! The water is going down!"

I looked where he was pointing. The water level in the engine room was dropping. Not very fast, but it was dropping. Then the alarm stopped.

The quiet was the best noise ever.

Isaac gave me the thumbs-up, and we climbed back into the saloon.

"I guess it fixed itself," Isaac said.

"I doubt it," I said, "but who cares. Let's go find my uncle."

I offered to keep lookout and let Isaac drive. He said the water and the panic fixed his feet, but maybe it would be good to change it up anyway. So he went behind the wheel, and I started up the mast.

"Jimi," he yelled, "wait a minute. Come here, please."

Isaac never says please.

I went back to the controls in the cockpit. Isaac pointed at the chart plotter.

"We're way off course," he said. "Should we go straight back and follow the old path, or should we just get started and work our way back?"

"We need to get back to the path," I said. "Uncle Tim is on the path. Go ahead and get started, and work your way back pretty soon. We'll see him if he's near here."

Isaac started the engine, put the *DUCK* in gear, and advanced the throttle. I headed for the mast.

"Wait a minute!" I said.

Isaac cut the throttle and took the *DUCK* out of gear.

"If we drifted off course, Uncle Tim drifted, too!" I said.

Isaac just looked at me.

"How far off course are we?" I asked.

Isaac pushed some buttons.

"Two hundred and sixty yards to the north," he said.

"And how long were we running around while the bilge alarm went off?"

"Got it," Isaac said. I could see the wheels turn.

"We stopped for about forty minutes. Your uncle could have fallen off the boat twelve hours ago," he said, "so he could have drifted...eighteen times as far as we did. That's...forty-six hundred yards, about. Forty-seven hundred, I suppose."

"That's a long way," I said.

"Almost three miles," Isaac said. "We need to look three miles north of the path!"

That was crazy.

But what could we do? Isaac put the *DUCK* in gear.

I could see pretty well after I climbed partway up the mast, and the sun was behind us, so the lighting was good, but I didn't see Uncle Tim. We agreed that Isaac would drive faster than we had before, because we were running out of daylight.

"That's the run," Isaac said. "We're back to where he turned last night."

I climbed down. We were done. Uncle Tim was dead. It was time to go home.

I just looked at Isaac and shrugged my shoulders.

"The sun hasn't set yet," Isaac said.

"So what do we do?" I said, looking around. The ocean was really big. Wide, wide open too. Now I got it.

"Grid search," Isaac said, "just like in the book."

"Fine," I said. Whatever.

"Except," Isaac said, "I was thinking. A person in the water wouldn't drift as far or as fast as a boat, because they don't stick up into the wind. So we'll split the difference."

Isaac put the *DUCK* in gear and spun the wheel.

"Get back up there, lookout," he said.

Isaac drove halfway back toward the turn point then turned right, straight toward the setting sun, and engaged the autopilot.

"There's not much time!" he yelled, pushing the boat faster than we had before. "We just have to try, though!"

I could see a line in the water ahead of us. On our side of the line, the water was gray. On the other side of the line, the water was green. There were a few sticks and bushes floating near the line, too. They were stuck in the tide rip!

"Isaac," I yelled, "follow that tide rip! Don't go right into it, but keep the boat near it!"

Isaac looked at me with a confused face, then looked at the water and turned off the autopilot. He understood.

I was scared. Really scared. Not only were we not able to find my dead uncle, but Isaac and I were about to spend a night at sea, alone, in a boat that was probably sinking. I almost slipped and fell off the boat last time I climbed up the mast, too. Mom would lose her little brother and her son in the same stupid way. I wondered if Uncle Tim even ever called her to tell her the new plans. Mom probably didn't even know where we were.

"There!" Isaac yelled.

I grabbed the mast and twisted around so I could see Isaac. Then I followed his arm out into the sea. Bobbing up and down, glowing in the red light from the sunset, was a little orange tent.

"It's a life raft!" Isaac yelled. "A life raft!"

Chapter 18:
Rescue!

"Isaac, STOP!" I yelled. "You're going to run right over him!"

Isaac looked at me and yelled, throwing his hands up, but no noise came out.

The raft was bright orange and had two round tubes around the bottom. There was a tent over the whole thing that covered everything. We couldn't see inside the tent. Maybe Uncle Tim wasn't even there. The bow of the *DUCK* just missed the life raft, and we hit it with the wide side of the boat, pushing it away and splashing it with water as we drove right past.

I needed to drive the boat. Isaac hadn't practiced driving enough, except out in the open where nothing mattered. He wasn't any good at stopping or turning or backing up or anything. I guess I hadn't practiced backing up, either. Maybe I wasn't a good driver, either.

"You should drive, Jimi!" he yelled. I was already moving back.

"Stand on the side!" I said, pointing. "I'll try and stop right next to the raft!"

Isaac moved about halfway up the left side of the boat to the widest part and grabbed the wires that held up the mast.

I turned the wheel hard to the left and put the *DUCK* in gear. The *DUCK* turned slowly to the left, but the turn was too big. We just circled all the way around the life raft.

Isaac looked at me. "I can't reach," he yelled.

Duh.

I tried turning the other way. The *DUCK* circled to the right, and then I straightened it out so we were pointed at the raft. I took the boat out of gear before we got there and tried to get next to the raft. Then I put the *DUCK* in reverse, for just a second, so we'd stop.

"I still can't reach!" Isaac yelled.

I could see that. The problem was, we were right next to the raft but I couldn't move the boat sideways. Boats don't go sideways. They either go forward straight, forward to the right, or forward to the left. Mary told me that the *DUCK* was pretty useless going backward, too. You couldn't make it go where you wanted.

I put the *DUCK* in forward and pulled away.

"Hey!" Isaac yelled, waving his arms.

"Hold on to the boat!" I yelled. "And don't fall in! I'm just going to go out and come in straight."

Isaac grabbed the mast wires again and looked at me. Then he gave me a thumbs-up.

I went forward in a straight line or as straight as I could make it. After just a few seconds, I checked over my shoulder. I could just barely see the life raft behind us. We were almost out of light.

I kept going forward for just a little bit longer, to give myself enough room to turn. There probably wasn't enough daylight left for a second try. Then I spun the wheel hard to the left.

I could just see the raft as we turned.

"Isaac!" I yelled. "Point at the raft!"

Isaac looked at me, then shrugged his shoulders and pointed, but with his finger.

"I can barely see you," I yelled. "Point bigger!"

He stared at me for a second, then turned forward and pointed with his whole arm.

Perfect.

I figured maybe Isaac did the right thing the first time, ramming the raft, except he didn't know how to stop. I really didn't want to miss again and try another pass in the dark.

I aimed the *DUCK* right at the raft. Right at it.

"You're going to sink it!" Isaac yelled.

"Just keep pointing!" I yelled back.

"Don't sink it!" he yelled again, but he got his arm up.

The *DUCK* was headed right for the raft. I could line up the mast and the bow and the raft. No way we would miss it. As we got closer, the raft started to disappear under the tall front of the boat.

"Jimi!" Isaac yelled. "Look out!"

I turned the wheel to the right and put the *DUCK* in reverse.

The life raft slide down the left side of the *DUCK*. I gave the boat a little more throttle, trying to get it to stop.

Isaac grabbed the top of the tent as it slid by and managed to hold on as the life raft slid past him. He was able to keep his grip on the tent while he walked back along the side of the boat.

Finally, the *DUCK* stopped in the water. I put the transmission in neutral and shut the motor off.

"Come here and help me hold this," Isaac yelled. "It's slipping!"

"One sec!" I yelled back, and dropped into the cabin. I grabbed some rope from one of the cabinets in the saloon and jumped back on deck.

Isaac took one end of the rope.

"Tie the other end off," he said, but I had already started. There was a cleat, which is a special boat part for tying things to, right near him on the side of the boat.

Isaac passed his end of the rope though a grab handle on the top of the tent, then handed it back to me. I tied it to the same cleat.

The life raft was tied to the boat. It was safe.

Isaac reached way over the rail and started pulling on the tent fabric. Most of it was tight, but he finally found a loose part and pulled. It flew up and over the top of the tent and down the other side, opening the entire side of the tent that faced the boat.

Inside the raft there were two big brown boxes and curled up between them, lying in a deep puddle of water, was Uncle Tim.

He wasn't moving.

Chapter 19:
Out of Danger?

I jumped right into the life raft with Uncle Tim. His lips were blue. Not a little blue, or red-blue, but blue. That was probably a bad thing. His skin was freezing cold, too.

"We've got to get him out of here!" I yelled. I knew that Isaac already knew that, but I yelled it anyway. Pretty stupid waste of time, really.

I tried to lift him up by the front of his shirt, but I could barely move him. He did groan a little, so that was good.

"I'll be back in a second," Isaac muttered.

I just kept trying to lift Uncle Tim. He was all tangled up in the boxes, and they were completely in the way.

I lifted his legs, but then his chest slipped down in the water and his face got wet.

He woke up, just a little. His left eye opened.

"Hi, Jimi," he said, "glad you're here."

Then his eye closed again.

I dropped his legs and tried to get his head out of the water. I couldn't move his whole body back to the edge of the raft, so I ended up having to kneel down under his head to hold it up. The water was very, very cold. But if I moved, Uncle Tim's head would go back into the water and instead of him dying at sea, he would be killed by his idiot nephew that could find a life raft in the middle of the ocean but couldn't lift a man onto a boat.

Lift.

"Isaac!" I yelled. "Isaac!"

"Yeah, Jimi?" Isaac said. He was right above me, on the edge of the *DUCK*. He had our tie-off line in his hands.

"The dinghy lifts!" I yelled. "We can lift him with the dinghy lifts!"

"Way ahead of you," Isaac said, "I just had to get the dinghy out of the way."

Holding on to the tie-off line, Isaac walked us to the back of the boat and retied the life raft. There were two hoisting arms at the back of the *DUCK* where Uncle Tim stored the dinghy. The dinghy wasn't there now,

Jimi & Isaac 2a:

and Isaac lowered one of the dinghy-hanging hooks into the life raft.

"Hook him," he said. "I'll haul him up."

I took the hook from Isaac, but…I just looked at Isaac. I was completely out of ideas. I was killing my uncle. I had to think.

But Isaac was gone, again.

I looked down at Uncle Tim's face. I could see he was breathing, because there was a little snot blowing in and out of his nose. I moved my eyes to look at his chest. It was moving a little too but not very much. I put my hand on his stomach. That seemed like a first-aid kind of a thing to do. It didn't seem to help. I was killing my uncle. I didn't know what to do, and it was killing Uncle Tim.

Right then, a big pile of green rope landed on my hand, right on Uncle Tim's gut.

"Tie it around his chest," Isaac said, "then we can lift him."

It was hard to hold Uncle Tim's head and pass the rope around his chest at the same time. I couldn't even see how to start.

"I'll come down and help," Isaac said, climbing over the side of the boat.

"NO!" I yelled. "No way! You stay on the boat!"

Isaac hesitated, then climbed back.

"Good call," he said. "You're right."

I finally had to get out from under Uncle Tim's head to get the rope around his chest. At first, I was real careful, but then his head slipped down and water washed up his face and into his nose and mouth.

He didn't even choke. That seemed bad.

I got the end of the rope under his back and up the other side, then went back and raised his head. Water ran out of his nose. He was still breathing, though. I could tell because the snot thing was way worse.

I slid my left leg under his head. Then I could reach both ends of the rope to tie a knot.

I was sitting in the water in the bottom of the raft and it was cold. It made it hard to remember how to tie the knot Mary showed me. Under and over and around...

"Last part is wrong," Isaac said. "Go back the way you came."

I looked at my knot. Then I looked at Isaac.

"The last part," he said, "go back the way you came. The rope crosses itself. It needs to lie next to itself."

I looked at my knot again. OK. Got it.

I fixed the knot and hooked in the dinghy lift.

"Hold on to him," Isaac said, and started to pull on the hoist line.

We got Uncle Tim on deck. Even that was stupid-hard. He was all floppy.

"Now what?" Isaac asked.

I didn't know. I was freezing.

Freezing.

"We need to get him warmed up," I said. "Give me the hose."

I sprayed Uncle Tim with hot water from the hose, but it got too hot and I didn't notice until Isaac got some on his foot. It seemed like everything I did hurt Uncle Tim.

"Let's get him inside the boat and head for shore," I said.

Isaac gave me the thumbs-up, and we dragged Uncle Tim forward through the cockpit and down the companionway into the saloon.

Uncle Tim's head bounced a little on the last step down. It made him open his eyes.

"Get the crates," he said. "Get the crates."

Then he closed his eyes again.

I looked at Isaac. He looked at me.

"From the raft," Isaac said finally.

Yep.

Chapter 20:
Safe?

"I've seen these before," Isaac said, nodding his head toward the boxes in the life raft, "there were some at the airport, with dogs in them."

"Can we just hook the handles?" I asked, pointing.

Each brown box had a handle in the top. The handles looked strong.

"It would be stupid to make a handle if you couldn't use it," Isaac said, reaching for the lifting rope. He jumped into the life raft. It was so dark now I could barely see him below the edge of the boat.

"Haul away," he said.

Jimi & Isaac 2a:

I pulled on the dinghy lift, and the top of the box appeared over the side of the boat. I kept pulling until it was as high as I could lift it. It was still hanging from the dinghy lift, but it was a little loose so it was banging around on the back of the boat.

Then we did the same with the other box and the dinghy lift on the right side of the boat.

Finally Isaac climbed back on deck.

"Are we good?" I asked. "Are we done?"

Isaac grabbed the line that was tied to the life raft and untied it, pulling on one end until it was coiled in his left hand.

"I don't want to mess with that anymore," he said as the life raft slowly drifted off.

"And I'll use this rope to tie the boxes so they don't swing too much."

I was glad Isaac wasn't wet and cold. Apparently wet and cold makes a person stupid. I should have thought of that.

He finished tying the boxes off.

The back of the boat didn't look right. The boxes were probably tied on OK, even though the knots were messy, but something wasn't right.

"Where's the dinghy?" I asked.

"It's gone," Isaac said.

I just looked at him.

"I was in a hurry," he said. "It didn't seem that important."

I looked at the sea around the boat. I couldn't see the dinghy anywhere, mostly because it was too dark.

"It wasn't," I said. "Important, I mean. Uncle Tim is important."

Isaac just stood there. I couldn't see his face. It seemed like I should say, "Good job" or something, but that didn't seem right, either. It was like I couldn't decide anything.

"After you, Cap'n," Isaac said, waving toward the companionway.

Captain?

Captains don't almost kill their uncles.

When we got back to the saloon, Uncle Tim was lying naked on the floor, except his pants were tangled around his feet and his shirts and jacket were all tangled around his right wrist. We tossed all his wet stuff outside. Isaac got a towel and dried the puddles off the deck. He tried to dry off Uncle Tim, but that was pretty weird so he didn't do a very good job.

"You need to change clothes," Isaac said. "You're dripping."

He mopped up the puddle at my feet again.

I started below, to our cabin.

"I'll get the boat going," Isaac said, "just follow the old path backwards?"

"Just follow the old path," I yelled, "as fast as you can!"

Jimi & Isaac 2a:

By the time I changed and threw my wet clothes up into the cockpit, the saloon floor was dry. It even felt warm on my bare feet. That gave me an idea.

"Are you good?" I asked Isaac. He was driving from the cockpit, playing with the throttles a little. Trying to go faster, probably.

"I'm fine, Cap'n," Isaac said. "Just driving the boat."

I ducked into Uncle Tim's cabin and grabbed all the blankets I could find and hauled them into the saloon.

I used another towel to finish drying Uncle Tim and the floor around him, and then I covered him with the blankets, leaving him lying on the bare, warm floor.

"Good idea," Isaac said, climbing down from the cockpit, "but maybe he needs to breathe."

I rearranged the blankets so Uncle Tim's face was exposed, then found one more clean towel and used it to make a pillow under his head. I couldn't see what else to do. At least I wasn't hurting him. Maybe things would get better.

"Jimi, wake up." Isaac was like six inches from my face. His breath was horrible. Not a little horrible, but like "teeth rotting in a stagnant pond" horrible.

"Wake up, Jimi," he said, still stinking. "You need to drive. I need to sleep."

Must be some sort of a dream, I figured. My sister, Janis, drives, but she's in high school. I don't drive, I'm just a kid. Two more years, three more years, sure, I'll drive then.

"I'll drive in two years," I told Isaac. That settled that.

"Jimi," Isaac said, "you need to drive now."

Then he pinched my arm, in the loose part in back, right below my shoulder.

He was too far away by the time I reacted. I couldn't reach him.

"I need to sleep," he said, shrugging, "in a bed. I fell asleep three times in the last hour trying to drive."

I looked around. It was dark, but from the lights from the radar screen, I could see where I was. I was on a tiny little sinking boat in the middle of the ocean. The open ocean.

I looked over the edge of the seat I was lying on. There was still a big pile of blankets on the floor.

"Your uncle is still breathing," Isaac said. "I checked every half hour."

I got my elbow underneath me and levered myself up to a sitting position.

"I'm sorry, Isaac," I said. "I meant to stay awake with you."

Isaac smiled and handed me the autopilot controls.

"You've got the con," he said.

Then he went forward to his bunk.

Isaac came up into the saloon just before sunrise.

"I'll make coffee," he said, putting the water pot on the stove.

"We don't drink coffee," I said.

Jimi & Isaac 2a:

He gave me the one-eye. "We do now. We need to stay awake, so we need the caffeine."

I figured I was going to start drinking coffee in five or ten years or so anyway. Isaac's dad says that college is impossible without coffee. Too bad we couldn't drink tea, though. Tea is good.

Isaac was reading the coffee label.

"There's no directions," he said, and looked at me.

I just shrugged.

He got out two coffee mugs and spooned some grounds into each one.

"How hard can it be?" he said, turning off the burner and adding hot water to the mugs. "Even stupid people drink coffee."

He handed me a mug. It actually smelled pretty good, so I took a sip. It was too hot, but it pretty much tasted like it smelled. Not bad, really.

Isaac looked at me and took a big gulp. He started choking right away, coughing and spitting and flicking his tongue in and out like a lizard. He dumped his cup into the sink and spit several times. Finally he grabbed a paper towel and used it to wipe off his tongue.

"Too hot?" I said, taking another little sip.

"Too gravelly," he said. "Like drinking a sandbox."

I started to laugh, but then the engine sped up, sputtered, and then died. It was really, really quiet after that.

Isaac and I just looked at each other.

Really quiet. It had been running for so long, I'd forgotten how loud the engine was.

...for so long.

"I forgot to change fuel tanks," I said. "We ran out of gas."

I jumped up the companionway to the cockpit and hit the START button on the engine control panel. Nothing happened. I did it again. Still nothing.

Isaac was standing in the companionway. He looked at me, bit his lower lip, then looked at the engine controls.

"You're in gear," he said.

Right.

I leaned back and moved the shifter lever to NEUTRAL, then hit the START button again. The engine growled as the starter turned, but it never caught.

I tried it again. Same deal.

I looked at Isaac again. He bit his lower lip and squinted, then looked at me.

"Did you switch the tanks?"

DUMB!

Isaac swung to the side while I jumped past him, then helped hold Uncle Tim's legs while I opened the hatch in the floor. I dropped into the engine room and changed the valves so we could pull fuel from the other fuel tank.

I started to crawl out of the engine room.

"Want me to double-check?" Isaac asked.

Jimi & Isaac 2a:

"No," I said, "it's pretty simple. Everything is color-coded."

Isaac didn't move or change his face.

I went back down and double-checked myself.

Back in the cockpit, I pushed START again. Again, the engine turned, but again, it didn't start. I tried four more times. Nothing.

I looked at Isaac. I was out of ideas. I couldn't think of anything. No bad ideas, no good ideas, nothing.

"The book," Isaac said, and retreated into the saloon.

He was already thumbing through the index by the time I started down the companionway. I decided to try my coffee again while Isaac read. It was usually worthless to look over his shoulder. He moved too fast.

By my second sip, he was turning to the middle of the book. I had just about given up on coffee altogether by the time he sat down and really started reading.

"This is insane," he said finally, leaving the book open in his lap.

I shrugged my shoulders.

"We need to bleed the fuel system," he said. "That means get all the air out."

I shrugged again.

He looked through the book again.

"We need to take the engine apart and put it back together, while we're trying to start it."

"No way!" I said. "Let me see."

Isaac handed me the book and pointed at the starting paragraph. I read through it. Isaac was exaggerating but not a lot. While the starter was running, we had to loosen fittings and then tighten fittings, and there would be gas spraying all over while we were doing it.

"Diesel fuel," Isaac corrected.

Right, not gas. Like it mattered. No way we could do this.

"We have to do it," Isaac said.

"We'll be killed," I said.

"We'll die anyway."

I thought about it for a while.

"I'll be in the engine room," I said. "You run the starter."

"*I'll* be in the engine room," Isaac said, "reading the book and fixing the stuff."

He was right.

Then Isaac looked up from the book and over my shoulder.

"Good morning, boys," I heard from behind us.

I spun around. Uncle Tim was sitting up, on the floor, wrapped in his blankets.

"Any coffee for me?"

Chapter 21:
More to Do.

It was nice to have Uncle Tim awake and talking to us. He made us tell him the whole story about looking for him and finding him. He really liked the whole "grid search" part. He thought that was pretty smart.

Then Uncle Tim had to walk Isaac through the coffee-making process step by step. Real coffee was actually awful, way more bitter and stronger than Isaac coffee.

Eventually Uncle Tim was ready to work on the motor. With him in the engine room, it took about thirty seconds. Maybe it wasn't as complicated as we'd thought.

"Where are we headed?" he asked as Isaac swung the boat around and returned to our old path.

"Town," I said. "We figured you needed a doctor. I mean, you need to see a doctor."

Uncle Tim looked down at his hands, meshed his fingers, turned them out, and stretched his arms.

"We thought you were dead," Isaac said, coming down the companionway stairs.

Uncle Tim smiled. "Not dead."

"Jimi kept giving up on you," Isaac said, "but I said we should keep looking."

Uncle Tim looked at me. I just shrugged my shoulders.

"It seemed pretty hopeless," I said. "I still don't understand how we found you."

"Yeah," Isaac said. "Pretty weird, you floating in a life raft. I didn't even know there was a life raft on this boat."

Uncle Tim smiled again. Then he jumped up.

"The otters!" he yelled. "How are the otters?"

Isaac and I just looked at each other.

"We haven't seen any otters," Isaac said.

"Did you see otters?" I asked. "Is that why you fell off the boat?"

"The crates," Uncle Tim said, yelling again. "They're in the crates from the raft! Where are they?"

"Tied to the back," Isaac said, pointing over his shoulder with his thumb.

Jimi & Isaac 2a:

Uncle Tim almost knocked him down. Isaac and I gave each other a look, then followed him.

Uncle Tim was pulling one box on deck. When he turned it, I could see there was a metal mesh door on the side facing away from the boat.

On the bottom of the heavy plastic box was a furry brown-and-black-and-gray animal. It was just a big pile. I couldn't see any shape or front or back or side.

Isaac reached in to poke it.

"Don't!" Uncle Tim said. "Leave it alone. It can bite your finger clean off."

"Jimi," Uncle Tim said, "go get some fish from the freezer. Bring a knife, too."

Then he started pulling the other box on board.

By the time I got back on deck, both otters were uncurled and looked like otters, except they were huge. As big as big dogs, except with short legs.

Uncle Tim took the frozen fish I gave him and whittled it like a stick, slicing off long, thin pieces. He'd take each piece and work it through the wire door, leaving a little sticking outside the box.

One otter figured it out right away and started eating the fish strips like bacon. The other otter was mostly sniffing around.

"Man, they stink," Isaac said.

He was right, too. Like the worst fish smell ever.

I looked in the cages and there was poop everywhere.

"Give me the hose, Jimi," Uncle Tim said.

I got the hose, and Uncle Tim sprayed it around the bottom of the boxes. I don't know how much it helped the otters, but it got stink all over the deck of the *DUCK*.

After the washdown, the second otter started eating its fish bars.

"They need to eat a lot," said Uncle Tim, "all the time, almost."

Uncle Tim washed the deck off with the hose.

"I need to go to bed," he said. "Can you guys drive?"

Isaac and I looked at each other.

Isaac shrugged.

"Sure," I said.

Uncle Tim smiled and handed me the hose.

"Wash your feet really well before you come below," he said. Then he dropped down the companionway.

When we got all cleaned up and into the saloon, Uncle Tim showed us the chart plotter. He'd created a new course line to follow.

"Otter Cove," he said, "we'll head directly for Otter Cove. We'll get there tonight right at dusk, anchor safely, then make it home tomorrow. How's that sound?"

"Cool," Isaac said.

"Sounds great," I said.

"It does sound great," Uncle Tim said.

He looked pretty tired.

Jimi & Isaac 2a:

"Feed the otters every hour, after you do your safety checks. Be real careful with the knife on deck while you're cutting the fish, and keep an eye on each other."

"Where will you be?" I asked. Isaac was already playing with the radar settings and adjusting our course with the autopilot.

"Like I said, I'm going to bed," Uncle Tim said. "Yesterday was rough. Wake me up when you see Otter Cove."

Then he gathered up his blankets, went into his cabin, and shut the door.

Chapter 22
Cause of the Problem.

"I think the otters are sick," Isaac said.

"They didn't eat the fish?" I asked. "They ate everything I fed them."

"No," Isaac said, "they ate everything. They just look messy and sad."

I didn't say anything for a while.

"You look pretty messy and sad," I said. "Are you sick?"

Isaac ran his hand through his hair. He probably should have washed his hand before he did that. Fish slime isn't a good hair gel. He was a filthy mess. I was, too, probably.

Jimi & Isaac 2a:

After watching the water for a few minutes, Isaac started in again.

"You know what kills a lot of otters now?" Isaac asked. "I read it in that book."

I just waited.

"Cats," he said. "Cats have a disease and they crap in the streets and it washes into the ocean and the otters get the same disease."

That was just silly, but Isaac is right sometimes. I didn't know enough to argue.

"You know what else cats kill?" he asked.

Man, was I tired. It looked like we had three more hours to go until we got to Otter Cove. I could be asleep in four, after we anchored and had some food. Maybe we could eat on the way, then we could be asleep in three and a half hours.

"Cats kill birds. Cats kill more birds than anything else."

Sure.

"Cats are death machines, pretty much. Death on four legs. Furry, silent death bringers. If you want more birds or more sea otters, you need less cats. Simple math."

Simple. Yeah, right.

"Figure out what we can eat," I said to Isaac. "If we eat before we anchor, we can go to sleep sooner."

"That," Isaac said, opening the cabinet under his seat, "is the best idea you've had today. Top ten ideas of all time, maybe."

Isaac found three cans of chili that were all the same and put them in the sink. Then he dug a can opener out of the silverware drawer and found a pan big enough to cook everything and put them in the sink, too.

"Everything's ready, Cap'n," he said. "Just give the command, and dinner will appear."

I smiled. Sometimes Isaac was pretty useful.

We looked at the water some more. I don't think either one of us saw anything. We were pretty tired.

"Indians," Isaac said finally.

"Drop it, Isaac," I said. "You don't know what you're talking about, and you're making everyone mad."

"No," Isaac said, "I do know what I'm talking about, and this is a big deal."

I just watched the water.

"Know what killed the Indians?" Isaac said.

"Cowboys," I said. "I saw it in a movie. Cowboys."

"Nope," Isaac said. "Mostly, nope."

The water looked the same.

"People came from Europe and Asia and moved here, and they brought diseases inside them that made the Indians sick."

"You're making me sick," I said. I knew he was right, but...

"Listen, Jimi," he said, "this is a big deal. If these otters are from Russia, and they swim down to California, they might take a new disease with them. If the California otters haven't ever had the Russian otter diseases, the California otters might all die."

Jimi & Isaac 2a:

"Like smallpox?" I said.

"Like smallpox," Isaac said. "Russian otterpox. These otters might kill all the otters America has left."

"Come on in," Uncle Tim yelled.

I opened his door.

"We're almost there," I said. "At Otter Cove."

He rolled over in bed and looked at me. I'd never seen anyone look so tired.

"Great job, Jimi," he said. "You're doing great."

"Dinner's ready, too," I said. "Canned chili."

Uncle Tim's eyes had already shut. He opened them again.

"I'm not hungry," he said. "I'll probably just sleep through the night."

"OK," I said, "but…"

"You guys know how to anchor," he said. "Mary taught you well."

"OK," I said, "but…"

"You'll do great," he said. Then he opened his eyes and smiled again.

"Jimi…"

"Yeah?"

"After dinner, after dark, finish the plan. Let the otters go."

I didn't say anything.

"Feed them first," Uncle Tim said, "give them some time to find their own food."

"But…"

"You'll do great, Jimi," he said. "Thanks."

Then he rolled over. I could barely see the back of his head behind the blankets.

I shut the door.

Chapter 23:
Not Over Yet.

"Isaac," I said, kicking his bunk, "get up. Let's get going."

It seemed like the *DUCK* was our boat now. It made sense for Isaac and me to make the decisions.

Isaac rolled over, I think. The edge of his blanket hung over the edge of his bunk. I tried to pull it off him.

"Get up," I said, a little louder.

Isaac grabbed the blanket before I could get the whole thing. At least he was awake.

"Are we going in today?" he asked. "I want to go in."

I did, too. It was time to get off the boat.

Last night, in the dark, the otters disappeared. They dropped out of the boxes, and we never saw them again. One splash each.

"Hey, Isaac," I said, "maybe the otters are still in the cove. We should go look."

That did it.

Once he dropped out of his bunk and left the cabin, I got up. It wasn't safe until then.

Isaac was all the way to the front of the boat when I got on deck. I ducked back below, then followed him.

"Here's your life jacket," I said, handing it to him. Then I got mine all zipped and buckled.

"Thanks," he said. "I don't see them."

I looked all the way around the boat. There weren't any other boats in Otter Cove and the water was really calm, but I didn't see the otters, either.

"They could be anywhere by now," I said. "Maybe they're up in the woods."

"Only river otters go into the woods," Isaac said. "Sea otters spend their whole lives at sea. Being in the boxes was probably the only time those things had been out of the water."

"The book?" I asked.

"Yeah," Isaac said. "It was a pretty good book. Lots of information."

We looked around some more. It sure was a pretty place. Real quiet.

"Jimi?" Isaac said.

"Yeah?"

Jimi & Isaac 2a:

"Let's go. I'll get the engine started; you get the anchor up. I'll make coffee after we start."

"Yeah," I said. "But maybe we should ask Uncle Tim."

"He was pretty tired yesterday," Isaac said. "We should let him sleep. He'll get up when the engine starts, if he wants to."

"Yeah," I said. "You're probably right."

Isaac made coffee after we were moving, and instant oatmeal.

I didn't drink most of my coffee. I waited until it was cold and Isaac wasn't looking, then threw it down the sink.

"Hey, coffee waster, I could drink that."

I looked at Isaac. I guess he *was* looking.

"Did you drink yours yet?"

He looked into the cup. At least he was holding it right. He looked like a coffee drinker.

"Almost," he said.

"Hey, Jimi?" Isaac said.

"Yeah?"

"I cooked; you do dishes. We should probably clean up before we get back to the docks."

Isaac, of course, meant that *I* should clean up before we got back to the docks.

But he was right. The boat was a mess.

"OK," I said. "I'll do dishes; you clean up the saloon and our cabin."

"Uh…"

"Don't touch my stuff," I said, "just get all your stuff gathered up, and try to straighten up this mess." I waved my hand toward the saloon.

Isaac moaned but rolled out of his seat. I gathered up the dishes.

I had everything soaped and scrubbed and went to rinse it all off. No water came out of the faucet.

"Hey, Isaac," I said, "now the water's broken."

"Go change the tank," he said.

Of course. Just like the fuel system. There were two water tanks. Uncle Tim had said there was plenty of water in just one, but we used a lot washing off the otters and cleaning the decks.

"You have the con," I told Isaac.

He nodded.

I found the ear protectors and dropped into the engine room. It didn't seem too bad this time. I crawled to the back, where the water tanks were, and switched the valves.

Then I went back upstairs to finish the dishes.

Still no water.

"Hey, Isaac," I said, and waved at the faucet.

"You probably didn't do it right," he said. "I'll fix it."

I know Isaac wasn't paying attention when Uncle Tim showed us how to switch tanks, but I didn't want to argue.

"I have the con," I said.

Jimi & Isaac 2a:

Isaac saluted, put on the ear protectors, and dropped into the engine room.

"Both tanks are empty," he said when he got back. He had been gone a long time.

I just looked at him.

"No way," I said. "They were both full when we left. Uncle Tim showed me. Showed *us*. They were both full."

"I know that," he said, "and now they're both empty."

He put the ear protectors back in their storage drawers, turned, and leaned back against the cabinet.

"The alarm," I said.

"I don't hear it," he said.

"No, the other night, when we thought we were sinking!"

He leaned back a little.

"Yep," he said.

"We weren't sinking," I said. "The tank leaked inside the boat."

"Yep," Isaac said.

"So we're fine."

"Yep. As long as we don't die of thirst," Isaac said. "Lot's of ways to die out here."

We could just see the harbor at the edge of the haze.

"We'd better get your uncle," Isaac said, "unless you think you can dock this thing."

"I'll get him," I said. "You have the con."

Isaac bowed at the waist, real low. I almost slapped him on the back of his head, but I was too tired.

"Uncle Tim," I said, knocking on his door.

Then I waited.

"Uncle Tim." I knocked louder. "We're almost back at the marina. Can you come on deck, please?

I didn't hear anything. The engine was running, so maybe that would be louder than Uncle Tim, but I think I would have heard him answer.

"Go in," Isaac said. He was right behind me.

I opened the door. Uncle Tim was lying on his belly, his face away from us. I ran to the far side of the bed.

"Uncle Tim!" I yelled, right in his face. Then I grabbed his shoulder and shook him. "Uncle Tim!" I yelled again. Isaac reached over and pinched the back of his arm, like he'd done to me two days ago.

Uncle Tim didn't move!

Isaac grabbed his shoulder and pulled, rolling him onto his back. Then he put his hand on Uncle Tim's chest.

"I can feel his heart beating," he said.

This was just plain stupid. All this work, all that we'd done, and now Uncle Tim was going to die right before we got him home?

Stupid wasn't even close. Double extra stupid.

"Hi, Mom," I'd have to say, "I killed your brother, but I'm fine."

That would be just great.

"Yeah, Mom, I love you, too, see you soon at the funeral."

Perfect. Oh man oh man oh man oh man.

"Jimi," Isaac said.

"What?" Uncle Tim's skin looked all white. I'd thought he had a tan.

"Jimi."

Uncle Tim's lips were all cracked, too. That probably meant something. Too bad I wasn't a doctor. Then I could help my uncle.

"Jimi!" Isaac yelled.

I looked up.

"Look what I found."

He was holding up a cell phone.

He held it out to me, and I took it.

"Check the recent calls," Isaac said.

Sure enough, the first name in the list was Mary.

"Maybe I should call 911," I said.

"I don't think that's for boats," Isaac said. "Try Mary first."

Isaac was right. As usual.

By the time we got to the marina, Mary was there waiting for us. There was also a fire truck and an ambulance and a whole crowd of firemen. They had all the boats moved away from the end of the dock, and all I had to do was go straight in.

I didn't want to ram them, though, and I ended up stopping just out of reach of the firemen, but I just put the *DUCK* in forward gear for a moment. Three firemen grabbed the front rail, and four more pulled the boat sideways until we were alongside the dock.

Mary jumped on board right after the first firemen grabbed the rail. She climbed down the companionway before I could get the engine turned off. Two firemen with huge toolboxes went in right after her, then two more right after them. There wasn't that much room in Uncle Tim's cabin. I don't know where they all went.

Isaac and I just sat in the cockpit. Nobody talked to us.

That was fine with me.

Two of the firemen finally left the boat. One of them roughed up my hair with his hand, which was totally unnecessary.

Mary came up right after them.

She pushed past the wheel and gave me the biggest hug I've ever gotten. My mom is the world hug champion, so I know all about hugs. This hug was huge. Her arms wrapped all the way around me three times.

Finally she let go of me and hugged Isaac. That didn't last long. Mom has never been able to hug Isaac successfully, either.

Mary sat back in the cockpit and wiped her eyes.

"I'm sorry, boys."

I didn't see that coming. I didn't say anything. Isaac may not have heard her. He didn't say anything.

"It looks like Tim will be OK," she said. "He's pretty dehydrated."

I looked at Isaac.

"We're out of water," I said. "The second tank leaked."

"Of course it did," she said. "It's not the first time."

"We let the otters go," Isaac said.

Mary's head dropped.

"In Otter Cove," Isaac said.

Mary leaned back and took a deep breath.

"I'm so, so sorry, boys."

I didn't get it.

Mary leaned forward and grabbed Isaac's hand with her right hand and mine with her left hand.

"I need to go to the hospital with Tim," she said. "Can you guys take care of yourselves tonight?"

"Sure," I said, "no problem."

She smiled at me. She was a good smiler.

"One problem," Isaac said.

What a jerk. Mary didn't need to hear our problems.

"We don't have any water," Isaac said.

Oops. That was a real problem.

Mary smiled. "You can get water on the dock," she said. "See the hose connections?"

I followed her pointing. We would have found them.

"And," she said, standing, "do you have enough food?"

I nodded.

"Lots of cans left," Isaac said. "I'm the reheat master."

Mary smiled and pointed at the buildings onshore. "The restaurant in that first building with the red door has great hamburgers. Go in there, and find this guy here…"

I followed her pointing to the crowd on the dock. A tall guy in a blue baseball hat waved at us.

"…and ROBERT WILL FEED YOU!"

Apparently the blue hat was Robert's. He gave us a thumbs-up. I gave him the OK sign. He gave me the OK sign back.

Two firemen came back on board and stood in the cockpit. Mary and Isaac and I had to move to the back of the boat. The two firemen got on either side of the companionway and reached down. When they straightened up, they each had an arm under one of Uncle Tim's armpits. They put their free hands under his head and lifted him straight out of the boat.

By the time Uncle Tim's butt was clear of the companionway, two other firemen had laid a stretcher out from the dock all the way to the cockpit. The firemen just slid Uncle Tim right onto the stretcher. Slick.

Uncle Tim waved at me, then waved me over.

I looked at the fireman that was working on him, and he nodded a little, so I went.

"Sorry, Jimi," Uncle Tim said.

I didn't answer. I still didn't understand.

"And thanks." Uncle Tim smiled. His lips were cracked and bleeding, but his skin looked better. Less papery.

"Get Isaac," he said, waving him over with his other hand. Uncle Tim had a needle in his arm that went to a big plastic bag full of water or something. It looked thicker than water. The fireman was holding the bag up over the stretcher.

"We need to go," the fireman said.

Isaac showed up.

"Wait," Uncle Tim said to the fireman, waving his hand again. I was worried he was going to pull the needle out.

He turned to us.

"Listen, boys," he said, "don't be blackmouth. Grow up. Be men. Go to sea."

"Good advice," the fireman said, wrinkling his chin and nodding at Uncle Tim.

Then the fireman turned to us.

"Back away, guys, we gotta go."

The whole dock cleared off instantly. It was like everyone just vanished. Even Mary.

Isaac and I just looked at each other.

Isaac shrugged.

We went below.

Chapter 24:
Back in the Air.

"How were the burgers?"

Mary's car was a lot nicer than Uncle Tim's car, and it wasn't full of boat crap and crap crap. Going to the airport was a lot nicer than coming from the airport.

"The burgers were great," Isaac said, from the backseat. "I had two."

I had my very own seat belt in the front passenger seat.

"Do you know what the best part was?" Isaac said. He was shouting a little. He didn't need to, but talking from the backseat is always a little iffy. Better to go loud.

Jimi & Isaac 2a:

"What's that?" Mary laughed. "I'm a little afraid to ask."

"Flush toilets," Isaac said. "Flush toilets are very nice."

Mary laughed again.

"Thanks for taking showers, too," she said.

"Our pleasure," I said. That had been my idea. I had to talk Isaac into it. He figured he could wait until he got home.

"We were lucky to be able to move your flights," Mary said. "We had to tell the airlines that your uncle got sick so they'd accommodate you. I think you'll be in first class."

"What's first class?" I asked.

"Front of the plane," Isaac said. "Caviar, croissants, foot massages. It'll be good, Jimi. Don't worry."

"How long will Uncle Tim be in the hospital?" I asked.

"I'll take him home tonight," Mary said. "He was pretty dehydrated and hungry."

I thought for a minute. "Yeah," I said, "he probably didn't eat or drink anything for two days."

"Except the coffee," Isaac yelled.

"Except a cup of coffee," I said.

Mary just looked at me for a second.

"I don't need the details," she said.

The car got quiet for a while.

"What's a blackteeth?" Isaac yelled.

"A what?" Mary tried to look at Isaac in the rearview mirror.

"A blackmouth," I said.

"Right," Isaac yelled, "blackmouth."

"It's a fish," Mary said. "Why?"

"Uncle Tim said we shouldn't be one," I said.

"What, exactly, did he say?" she asked quietly.

"He said," Isaac yelled, "that we should be men and go to sea and not be blackmouth."

Mary stared straight ahead and just drove for a second.

"Well," she said, "that's pretty good. Maybe the smartest thing Tim's ever said."

"What?" Isaac yelled from the backseat.

"Can you hear me?" Mary raised her voice a little.

"Roger!" Isaac yelled.

"The biggest salmon around here are the Chinook. They're easy to identify when you catch them, because they have black gums. Other salmon have white gums."

"So it's about flossing?" I asked. That was stupid.

"Just wait," Mary said, "let me finish."

Isaac shifted as far forward as he could.

"Baby Chinook salmon are born in freshwater streams high in the mountains. They spend their first year in the streams. Then they migrate to the ocean and grow up somewhere in the middle of the Pacific Ocean. When they return to the streams four years later to spawn, they're the biggest, strongest fish around. They grow huge. When they come back, big and strong, everyone calls them kings."

Mary shifted her body a little and changed into the right lane. Traffic was getting heavier ahead.

"But the sports fishermen can't catch the salmon in the ocean; they're too far from shore. So the fish managers take some of the baby Chinook from the hatchery and hold them in pens until they're too old to migrate."

"Too old? Like not strong enough?" Isaac asked. I didn't understand her either.

"No," Mary continued, "the fish only have the instinct to go to sea for a short while. If you hang on to them for just a little extra time, if you keep them in the rivers and treat them like babies, they never really grow up. They just hang around for the rest of their lives. They don't get very big, and the fishermen catch them year round."

"Those are the blackmouth," I said. "Fish that don't grow into kings?"

Mary smiled at me.

"You got it," she said.

"I don't want to be a king," Isaac said, sitting back in his seat. "I want to be the emperor."

Chapter 25:
Everyone Knows Tim.

"I'll kill him!"

I didn't get it. Mom never kills anything. She catches mosquitoes and carries them outside to be free. She doesn't even like to shout. Now she was shouting about killing.

"I'll strangle him until his ears fall off!"

Dad was laughing.

Isaac reached for two more pancakes before Mom grabbed the platter and went back to the stove.

"Saint Timonius strikes again," Dad yelled, holding his fork in the air.

"That jerk!" Mom said, dropping the platter in the middle of the table. Four new pancakes. I got the top two.

"Which jerk?" Janis said, wobbling into the kitchen. Janis is often the slowest one to understand something. She tries hard, but she has limited potential.

"My little brother!" Mom yelled. She kept making pancakes, though.

"Saint Timonius?" Janis said. "I thought all that was over."

Wait.

What?

"All that what?" I asked. "Who's Saint Timonius?"

Janis grabbed a plate and sat next to Isaac. She slid two pancakes off the platter.

"Please pass the butter, Isaac," she said.

He kept eating. He probably didn't hear her. Usually only dogs and insects can hear her voice.

Janis reached across Isaac and grabbed the butter. When she pulled back, all the syrup from around Isaac's mouth was gone.

"He still has my suitcase," Isaac said. "He should send me my suitcase."

Janis smeared out a big blob of butter on her cakes.

Isaac shrugged and took a big bite of pancake. The syrup around his mouth reappeared.

"Who's Saint Timonius?" I asked, again.

"Is he in jail?" Janis asked.

"Not yet," Dad said. "Looks like he might get away with this one."

"HELLO!" I yelled.

Mom and Dad and Janis stopped talking and looked at me. Isaac took another bite of pancake.

"Who's Saint Timonius?" I asked for the third time.

"A dead man," Mom said, reaching for the platter.

That cracked Dad up.

"It makes perfect sense that you don't know," Janis said. "It's so hard for little children to keep up with family news, what with their early bedtimes and all."

Dad raised his fork again. He better get some pancakes on his plate or he was going to miss out. "Saint Timonius is your Uncle Tim. He's the patron saint of 'do as I say, not as I do.'"

"And will soon be dead." Mom said. She seemed to be running out of gas on the "killing Uncle Tim" issue.

"He gets people to give him money," Dad continued, "to supposedly solve ecological problems, then he does something big and stupid and gets in trouble, and then uses the trouble to raise more money. He calls himself an activist, but really he's an agitator. A professional agitator. He makes trouble for a living."

"How can you not know this?" Janis said. "Everyone knows this."

"Except he said he was done," Mom said. "I never would have let you boys go if I thought he would do this. Never."

She looked really upset. Mom says that when people are really mad, they're usually mad at themselves, mostly. I think she was mostly mad at herself.

"Mary said he was done, too," Dad said. "He lied to everyone."

"Unless Mary lied to cover for him," Janis said.

"Mary wouldn't lie," Dad said.

"Mary said she was sorry," Isaac said.

"I think we're all sorry," Mom said, putting the platter back on the table. Four fresh pancakes. Dad got the top two.

Chapter 26:
No Jail.

Uncle Tim didn't go to jail. Smuggling otters is a pretty big crime, but since they couldn't find who left the otters in the life raft, they couldn't prove that Uncle Tim was in on it. He just kept saying he saw the raft, didn't know what it was, and fell in checking it out. Everybody knew he was lying, but they couldn't prove it. So he didn't go to jail.

Mom and Mary talked on the phone for a long, long time. Mom cried mostly. I don't think I'm going to see Uncle Tim or Mary anytime soon. I'm OK with that.

Jimi & Isaac 2a:

Nobody saw the otters again, as far as I know. I keep an eye out for news stories about California otters having a Russian otterpox epidemic.

Uncle Tim was right about one thing, though. I don't want to be a blackmouth. I want to be a king. Isaac still wants to be the emperor.

END

About the Author

Phil Rink is an author, a professional mechanical engineer, an inventor and entrepreneur, a licensed ship's captain, and a private pilot. He also has run science fairs and coached kids for years in sports (mostly soccer) and for Science Olympiad teams.

Review our Books!

Help others find Jimi & Isaac Books.

Read Phil Rink's other Jimi and Isaac books!

Jimi & Isaac 1a: School Soccer
Jimi & Isaac 2a: Keystone Species
Jimi & Isaac 3a: Mars Mission
Jimi & Isaac 4a: Solar Powered
Jimi & Isaac 5a: The Brain Injury

Be a FAN:

www.facebook.com/Jimi.Isaac.Books

Made in the USA
Lexington, KY
27 April 2016